"There's something you should know, Will."

Will stiffened, the angry panic shooting through him. What could Taylor possibly say to make things right? Here they were, stranded in the middle of nowhere, with no chance of reaching his daughter, and Taylor somehow managed to find humor in the situation?

"That mudslide did the trick. It threw us to the other side of the river, where Andi is."

Face burning, Will ducked his head. "I'm sorry. I don't usually lose my cool like that. I never intended to scare you."

"It's okay," Taylor said softly. "You're worried for her. I understand." A look of surprise moved through her expression. "And you didn't scare me." Her blue eyes met his. "I'm not afraid when I'm with you."

The weight of Taylor's admission hung in the air between them. Something in her tone—awe or wonder, maybe?—unsettled Will. He watched her face, an ache spreading through him at the wounded vulnerability in her eyes...

April Arrington grew up in a small town and developed a love for books at an early age. Emotionally moving stories have always held a special place in her heart. April enjoys collecting pottery and soaking up the Georgia sun on her front porch.

Smoky Mountain Danger

APRIL ARRINGTON

ISBN-13: 978-1-335-42702-1

Smoky Mountain Danger

This edition published by arrangement with Harlequin Books S.A.

For questions and comments about the quality of this book, please contact us at CustomerService@Harlequin.com.

Love Inspired
22 Adelaide St. West, 40th Floor
Toronto, Ontario M5H 4E3, Canada
www.Harlequin.com

Printed in U.S.A.

Be strong and of a good courage...
for the Lord thy God, he it is that doth go with thee;
he will not fail thee, nor forsake thee.
—*Deuteronomy* 31:6

For Billie Ann.

Chapter One

Will Morgan, wrapped around his daughter's finger from the day she'd been born, had caved in to her requests often over the years…but he'd never agreed to anything as unpredictable or potentially dangerous as a weeklong journey down Tennessee's wild and scenic Bear's Tooth River.

"It's not too late to turn around, you know?" Will palmed the steering wheel of his truck and eased around a steep curve, the engine rumbling louder as the truck ascended the steep mountain. "We could drive back down the mountain, call Jax and tell him we changed our minds. Spend the week at one of the campgrounds we used to go to." He glanced at his daughter in the passenger's seat. "You used to love fishing at Badger's Crossing. We could be there within the hour, if you'd like?"

Andi, staring ahead silently at the bluet wildflowers lining the curving road in front of them, turned her head and locked her brown eyes with his. "I knew you'd try to back out."

Will flexed his jaw and returned his attention to the road. Drumming his fingers against the steering wheel, he sifted carefully through his thoughts for the right words. "I'm not backing out. I'm merely suggesting—"

"That we back out."

He stifled a sigh. Since Andi had hit her teens, every conversation with her had become a potential land mine, and when she'd turned seventeen two months ago, prying more than five words from her at a time had become almost impossible. Until Jax Turner, a sixty-year-old river guide and family friend, had mentioned he planned to lead a new tour of the Smokies down the rarely traveled white water of Bear's Tooth River.

Andi had latched on to the idea and had pleaded with Will for over a month to reserve the two seats still available on the one raft Jax, who ran a small business of river tours, had advertised. Jax's river trip had been the one and only topic she'd allowed him to broach with her without stoic resistance.

"The last thing I want to do is back out, Andi," Will said quietly. "I'm just concerned about the river. Jax has only run it a couple times and I've never run it at all. It's risky, and I don't like the idea of not knowing what lies ahead."

She continued staring at the road, her mouth barely moving as she spoke. "Then I don't understand why you agreed to it in the first place."

That was easy, Will thought, slowing the truck as

they reached the mountain's summit. "Time." He eased the truck over to a small graveled clearing, parked between a large SUV and a small sedan and cut the engine. A broad river flowed several feet in front of a large boulder that served as a drop-off point. "I wanted to spend time with you—to talk, to laugh, to just enjoy each other's company again for once."

Andi's mouth tightened. "You could have that anytime, if you didn't work every single day."

"Someone's got to pay the bills," he said quietly. Pay for construction jobs wasn't steep nowadays, but the gigs were easy to come by and he needed every one he could get to put Andi through college in another year.

"I know. But what good's a house if no one's ever in it when you come home?"

Will closed his eyes, a fresh surge of guilt moving through him. "Andi—"

"Besides," she said, "you don't always know what lies ahead, anyway." She looked at him then, her eyes meeting his, then roving over his expression. "You didn't know Mom would walk out on us, did you? And even when you did, you couldn't stop her."

Will drew his head back at the anger flashing in her wounded eyes. It'd been sixteen years since his wife, Heather, had left him and abandoned Andi, and he'd hoped the passage of time would help ease Andi's pain. Instead, Andi's anger had only increased—as had her resentment for him, it seemed.

He moved to speak, but there was nothing he could say, so he remained silent and returned her stare.

Andi unsnapped her seat belt, opened her door and

got out of the truck. Moments later, the truck's tailgate lowered with a squeak and bags rustled as Andi lugged them across the bed of the truck.

Will got out of the truck and dragged a hand over the tight knot at the back of his neck. The sound of rushing water filled the rocky clearing and expanse of open sky on either side of the river. It was a surprisingly cool morning for summer in Tennessee, but the fragrant scents of pine, wildflowers and fresh earth filled his lungs and lifted his spirits a bit. Will had grown up in this neck of the woods, so the Smoky Mountains had always felt like home to him.

"'Bout time y'all made it." Jax, standing by a large raft anchored by the boulder, sauntered over and thrust out his hand. "I was beginning to think you'd changed your mind."

"He tried to," Andi bit out. She strolled by, a bag slung over her shoulder as she headed for the raft.

Jax winced and one corner of his mouth tipped up in a slight smile. "She giving you trouble already?"

Will pinned a smile in place—one he'd had to dredge up more often than not lately—and shook Jax's hand. "Seems that way." He strolled to the truck bed and retrieved a couple of bags of supplies. "Thanks for saving the last two seats on the raft for us. If nothing else, I hope a week trapped together on a raft will give me some time with her."

Time to try to get Andi to understand how much he loved her and, hopefully, bridge the distance between them. A distance that grew wider and more impassable each day.

Jax grabbed a bag, too. "Come on. I'll introduce you to the rest of the group."

Will followed Jax over to the smooth boulder where a young man and woman stood, shrugging on life jackets.

"Meet Beth and Martin Hill," Jax said, sweeping his arm toward the couple. "Recently married. Came up from Florida for their first family vacation this year."

Will smiled, a sincere one this time, and held out his hand. "Congratulations."

Martin shook his hand firmly, a wide grin appearing as he glanced at his wife. "Thanks. Couldn't be happier, or more eager to hit the river, huh, honey?"

Beth nodded. "I've been looking forward to this for weeks. We've been on a few rafting trips before but never one as exciting as this one promises to be." She fastened the last buckle on her life jacket and raised her brows at Jax. "Are the views along this stretch as impressive as they say?"

Jax laughed. "Oh, don't nothing compare to the sunsets out here, and after we camp the first night and run the second set of rapids, there's a waterfall that'll take your breath away." He glanced at Will. "Course, we'll need to put the raft to shore at Hawk's Landing so we don't head over the falls downriver."

Will nodded, his smile dimming. "That's a definite."

"Speaking of the falls," Jax said, motioning toward a woman who stood several feet away, her back to them as she studied the landscape ahead. "We got a guest who's looking especially forward to those. Taylor? Come on over and meet your rowing partner." Jax glanced at Will and grinned, speaking in low tones. "Andi told me on the phone when y'all booked the trip that she preferred a seat up front, so I figured you needed a partner, and I think Taylor will be a good one."

Will frowned, squinting against the sharp rays of the morning sun as the woman strolled across the rocks toward him, stopping when she reached his side. Blond hair, dark blue eyes and a wary expression met his.

"Taylor's a photographer," Jax said. "She's eager to get the perfect picture of the Smokies."

She smiled slightly. "I don't think there's such a thing as perfect, but something close to it would do."

Will studied the camera she held with both hands, her graceful fingers curled tightly around the edges. "I'm Will—" he motioned toward Andi, who eyed them closely "—and that's my daughter, Andi. You and I are rowing partners, it seems." He lifted his hand in invitation. "It's nice to meet you."

Taylor studied his hand, her eyes moving from his palm and up his arm to his face. Her gaze—strangely vulnerable and apprehensive—darted away from his as she lifted the camera with a rueful smile, seeming to motion that her hands were full. "It's nice to meet you, too."

"Well." Jax rubbed his hands together briskly. "Let's get this show on the road."

Will lowered his hand and watched as Taylor joined Beth and Martin as they secured bags into the raft. Andi eyed Will from the other side of the boulder, then walked to the raft, hopped in and took her seat at the helm.

Will shook his head and trudged toward the raft, the uncomfortable churn in his gut reminding him the opportunity to back out had passed.

Taylor Holt had braved dangerous paths before, but the fierce churn of white water below the bank of Tennessee's Bear's Tooth River shot ice through her veins—especially since the first day of rafting had been relatively calm and uneventful.

"Glad you don't run 'em blind."

She tore her attention from the violent currents and focused on the man towering by her side on the rough-hewn overlook. "What?"

"The rapids." He dragged a broad hand through his dark hair, his toned biceps flexing below the short sleeves of his damp T-shirt with the movement, and pinned his dark gaze to hers. "Some people don't scout. They dive headfirst down these waters and don't give a thought to what lies ahead. Good to see you're not one of them."

Taylor tried to smile, but her mouth tightened into a thin line instead. She studied the kindness in his brown eyes, the soft contours of his lips and relaxed posture. During the initial twelve miles of their rafting journey and one peaceful night of camping by the river with the rest of the group, she'd picked up additional bits of comforting information about Will Morgan. The single father approached rapids with caution, admired peaks of the Smoky Mountains along calm stretches of water and patiently tried to engage his teenage daughter in conversation despite her uninterested glances and monotone responses. All of this should've eased the tension tightening Taylor's grip on her camera.

But the hardest lesson Taylor had learned in her thirty-five years of life was that a handsome face and welcoming expression could mask an insatiable desire to inflict pain, and not only had this led her to refuse Will's polite handshake yesterday, but it'd also led her to keep a healthy distance between them at all times.

She lifted her camera, adjusted the aperture for a greater depth of field and snapped pictures of white water boiling around bone-splintering boulders. "I like to see what I'm getting into."

Especially since she hadn't seen the danger coming with her late husband. On the surface, Preston Holt had been a successful real-estate agent, selling beautiful homes to hopeful families while seeking to establish one of his own. But beneath his calm exterior, he'd hidden a resentful nature and violent temper. Both had become increasingly evident after he and Taylor had married. Until the morning she…

Hands shaking, Taylor lowered the camera and pointed toward one side of the rapids. "There's a hole on the right. And we'll need to steer clear of—"

"You're joking, right?" Will tipped his head back and narrowed his eyes at the gray clouds hovering low among the mountain range. "It rained five out of seven days last week and showered for an hour after our raft hit the river this morning. That water's gotta be hitting three by now."

"What's hitting three?" Andi, Will's daughter, climbed the slippery overlook in their direction, her rafting helmet in one hand.

"The water," Will said absently, cupping Andi's elbow and steadying her. "It's running three thousand cubic feet per second. Maybe more."

"All the better for an exciting ride." She shrugged off his touch, walked past him and stood beside Taylor. "Whatcha think, Taylor? It's at least a Class IV, ain't it?"

Taylor nodded. "At least."

"It's pushing Class V." Will's tone hardened. "The water's fast and high. Too high."

"Not for you." Andi peered up at Taylor, excitement in her brown eyes, and smiled. "Or Taylor. You've run Class V rapids before, haven't you?"

Taylor studied the teen's hopeful expression. Andi's smile, the first Taylor had seen her flash on the trip, was sincere and brightened her expression. The defiant look she'd given Will yesterday had vanished a bit more with each mile they'd traveled downriver. Andi was much more approachable when she let down her guard.

Taylor smiled back. "Yeah. A few."

"You're not afraid," Andi announced, facing the rapids. The humid summer breeze tugged a long strand of brown hair free of her braid as she studied the river. "You're itching to run 'em."

Taylor tensed, realizing Andi was half-right. She did long to run the rapids—but not because she wasn't afraid. The swift currents crushing against carved earth terrified her, but feeling anything other than the numb despair she'd carried for five years would be a welcome relief. And navigating the roaring waters would drown out the thoughts needling the back of her mind…at least for a while.

"I'd like to take on the challenge," Taylor said. "But not just for the action. I'm a travel photographer, and *Wild Journey* magazine only buys photos of the most impressive, rarely traveled trails. From what I've heard, they're after shots of this river in particular." She pointed downriver at a bend where steep green mountains converged, swallowing the rapids and obscuring the view. "According to Jax, the best falls are miles ahead and I need the shots." She wagged her camera in the air. "Otherwise, I can't make a sale."

"And if we don't hightail it over these rapids soon, we won't make it to the next campsite by nightfall. We just got to be sure to shore up at Hawk's Landing before we hit the falls." Jax, their gray-bearded river guide, ambled up onto the overlook, propped his hands on his lean hips and grinned. "Ain't nothing like pushing through one last set of chaos before resting peaceful under the stars."

Taylor smiled. Jax's easygoing nature and good sense of humor made it hard not to like him. He looked to be in his early sixties, had a deep appreciation for nature and reminded her a lot of her first foster father, Kyle. She'd lived for three months with Kyle and his wife as a teen during a time when she used to dream of finding a family of her own. Years before she met Preston and years before his death, after which she spent each passing year alone.

"It's the chaos part that bothers me," Will said, a half-hearted smile appearing. "This is the roughest stretch of water I've seen in a while. We'd do better to hike back upriver and call it a d—"

"No way." Andi huffed and glared at Will. "Why'd you go through with this if all you planned to do was drag me back home the second day?"

Will frowned. "Watch your tone, please. I agreed to this trip to spend time with you, but this—" he swept a muscular arm toward the rough rapids "—was not part of the agenda."

"We've run tough rapids before—plenty of times."

"None like these," Will said, lowering his voice on his next words. "I'm just watching out for you."

"You're saying you don't think I can pull it off. Finding an excuse to go home and get back to work. That's what you're doing." Andi glanced at Taylor, her cheeks turning red as she whispered, "I can't wait till I turn eighteen next year. I'm leaving the second I do, no matter what he says." Eyes glistening, she started walking back down the overlook. "I should never have come out here with you."

"Andi!" A muscle ticked in Will's jaw as he called after his daughter, then smiled tightly at Taylor. "Sorry about that. She's..."

Hurt. Afraid. Aching for attention. Taylor recognized the signs. She shook her head. "It's okay. I didn't mean to encourage her."

But you did. Will didn't say the words, but the accusation in his dark gaze screamed the sentiment. He shoved his hands in his pockets, staring as Andi rejoined Beth and Martin at the raft. The lines of pain creasing Will's forehead made Taylor long to reach out and offer comfort. Cup her hand around the stiff set of his broad shoulders and squeeze.

Instead, she gripped her camera tighter, lifted it and snapped another photo of the rapids.

"You brought her to the right place, Will." Jax eased past Taylor and clamped his hand on Will's shoulder. "Those rough waters are good at pushing people closer together. Closer to God, too."

Taylor followed Jax's line of sight as his gaze moved across the river, up the lushly forested mountain peaks, and lingered on the low-hanging fog and clouds.

"Those are His waters." A note of pride entered Jax's tone. "His smoke. Know what my ol' pops used to say?" At Will's silence, he continued. "Used to say, when the world broke a man, all he had to do was come to God's land and let Him know he's here. Peace is in this place—all around. You just got to look for it."

Taylor's throat tightened. She swallowed hard, blinked past the wet blur along her lower lashes and listened to the rhythmic crash of free-flowing water against rugged stone. From where she stood, she saw nothing but violent rapids, the threat of rain and a less-than-welcoming rowing partner.

Will moved out of Jax's comforting grip and faced them. "In the past, I always ran a river first before bringing Andi with me. That way I'd know what I was getting her into." His dark eyes met Taylor's briefly. Then he cast Jax a questioning look. "Can you guarantee that we'll get my daughter safely over those rapids?"

Taylor looked down and dragged the toe of her waterproof sneaker across the dry rock.

Jax's brow furrowed as he shook his head. "You've lived in these mountains long enough to know that I can't guarantee you anything. No one can. I'm leading this tour, but we decide as a group whether or not to turn back." He rocked back on his heels and drew in a heavy breath. "But what I can tell you is that I don't think you're gonna gain any ground with Andi if you turn back now. That sun'll set and the rain'll roll in before we'd be able to hike back more than a mile and who knows where we'd end up spending the night then. We'd be at the mercy of whatever's roaming around us, and they don't call this river Bear's Tooth for nothing." He shook his head. "There's no way to portage past these rapids. Only way through is on the water. We either take a chance on running 'em, shore up at Hawk's Landing and camp safely for the night, or we hike back and chance getting lost in the dark."

Will stared at the rapids, remaining silent, then headed back down the steep, rocky bank. "I'll check with Beth and Martin," he said over his shoulder. "See what they want to do. If they're gung ho on tackling the rapids, I'll agree to it—but only if the majority of the group votes to proceed."

Taylor watched him take long strides down the bank to the raft, which was tied off at a calm section of the river. She studied his handsome features as he spoke to Beth and Martin and glanced at Andi, who stood, arms crossed, several feet away.

"Why'd he bring her here?" Taylor asked softly.

Face heating, she apologized to Jax. "It's none of my business and I don't mean to pry. But if Will lives here and knows how dangerous this river is, why'd he bring her?"

Jax grunted, the sound half regretful and half frustrated. "She's restless. Angsty like a lot of teens, you know? But she's angrier than most. Been pushing Will away, threatening to leave. Took off on him for a week two months ago. Gave him a good scare."

"And her mom?"

"Ain't in the picture. Never has been, really." Jax rolled his shoulders and sighed. "I've known Andi since she was small enough to cradle on one arm. Back in the day, she and Will used to rock climb and run rapids all the time, but Will works long hours now. Andi's good at it. Loves the water. When I told her I was setting up another run down these rapids, she begged to come and talked Will into it. He's so desperate to hold on to her he'd agree to just about anything right now."

Taylor watched Will move to Andi's side by the water, her grip easing on her camera.

"And you?" Jax asked.

She bit her lip as he peered into her eyes. "What about me?"

"You booked a ticket for this ride, too. Why'd you come out here?"

Her breath quickened and she moved to speak twice before finally saying, "To take photos. I came for the falls."

Jax smirked. "Yeah. You keep telling yourself that."

Taylor stiffened as he turned and walked away.

"And while you're at it," Jax added, working his way down the steep rocks, "pray we make it through those rapids in one piece. If anything happens to Andi, Will's gonna come after us both."

This trip had been a mistake, and every mile they traveled added another.

Will narrowed his eyes against the spray of cool water and firmed his grip on the paddle as the raft bounced along choppy water downriver. His gut sank further each time Andi's long braid, lifting and lowering with the jerky movements of the raft, slapped against her back in front of him.

"How's the view from up there?" Jax shouted from his position in the back of the raft.

Andi laughed. The sound echoed off the rocky banks that pinned them in on both sides. "It's gorgeous!"

Will's skin prickled when the first set of rapids emerged into view. He should never have agreed to bring Andi down this river without running it first—no matter how badly she'd wanted to come. "Sit lower, Andi, and use the foot cups. We're about to hit the rough stretch."

"I'm fine." Andi glanced over her shoulder, her eyes bright with excitement below her helmet, and grinned at Taylor, who was seated beside Will. "The rapids are a thousand times bigger down here than they were from the bank."

Taylor nodded. She maintained her focus on the rapids ahead, but her knuckles turned white around her paddle. "They always are."

"Second thoughts?" Will asked.

She met him head-on, determination flashing in her blue eyes and a blank expression on her face. "No. Just excited."

She was lying. The tight set of her pink mouth and the flush along her smooth freckled cheeks gave her away. Another time, another place, he'd be tempted to pursue the truth. Maybe even attempt to delve deeper into her past and discover the source of the shadows lurking in those beautiful blue eyes. Something—or someone—had put those shadows there, and he couldn't help but wonder what secrets she was hiding.

But that had always been his biggest flaw, hadn't it? Falling hard for a troubled woman. Wanting to protect and heal. No matter how hard he'd tried, he'd failed with Heather. And she had not only divorced him, she'd abandoned Andi, too.

Clenching his jaw, Will faced forward, ignoring the pretty ripple of Taylor's blond hair below her helmet and the brush of her warm forearm against his as she paddled. Andi came first. Always. There was no room in his life for a woman, especially one whose hardened demeanor reminded him more of Heather than he felt comfortable admitting.

"They do look a lot faster up close," Beth said, her voice shaking slightly behind Will. He couldn't tell if it was from excitement or fear.

"No bigger than Old Bend." Her husband, Martin,

seated beside her, laughed. "And we tamed that beast the second we hit water, didn't we, baby?"

Despite his anxiety, Will grinned. Martin and Beth, young and in love, were eager for adventure, and the white water swirling and crashing along bends and drops offered excitement the vacationing couple couldn't resist. They'd enjoyed traveling the river yesterday and had looked even more forward to today's rougher journey.

"Adrenaline pumping back there yet?" Will asked. He knew the feeling well. Missed it from his early days of braving rapids and hiking rough terrain.

"You know it," the couple called out in tandem.

Their energy was contagious. Taylor laughed with them, the brief expression of delight on her face catching Will's eye despite his best intentions to keep his focus elsewhere.

The splash of waves grew louder, and the raft, positioned sideways, drifted toward the mouth of the rapids.

"We're up," Jax shouted. "Paddle forward!"

Five paddles hit the water. Jax, Martin, Beth, Taylor and Will paddled together, pointing the nose of the raft into the rapids that carried them over the first thrash of white water.

"Stop and hold!"

At Jax's command, Will lifted his paddle and held on to the raft, his heart hammering against his ribs as Andi hunkered down. Swift currents lifted the raft, yanked it over a smooth underwater boulder, then plunged it, nose-first, into turbulent waters below.

Andi flopped forward against the raft's nose, as did

the rest of them, pressing together in a heap as the raft dropped into lower rapids, then reared back up, slinging them all backward in a tangle of paddles and limbs.

Cold water splashed high in the air, slapping their cheeks and pouring into the bottom of the raft. The raft rocked, tilted, rose and lowered. Dodged sharp rocks and smooth boulders. Over and over, until the current shot it free of the first set of rapids and lowered it onto a brief stretch of smooth water, tugging them farther downriver.

Andi sprang up, tilted her head back and released a triumphant yell. Her energetic cry, heavy with excitement, echoed along the banks of the river and reverberated against the rugged mountain range. She looked back at Will, the sheer joy on her face making his breath catch.

"That was amazing, Dad!" Water droplets fell from her helmet, coursed down her cheeks and pooled at the corners of her bright smile. "Absolutely amazing!"

And just like that, it was worth it. The grave misgivings he'd experienced when he finally gave in to Andi and booked the trip, the uncomfortable argument in the truck's cab yesterday morning, her monotone responses upriver and angry outburst on the overlook. All of it. Just for the sight of that one smile. A glimpse of the bighearted, joyful girl he'd known Andi to be years ago.

"Yeah," Will rasped, his throat closing as he smiled. "Amazing."

"Paddles up, you heroes!" Martin lifted his paddle, urging everyone to high-five paddles above the raft.

Laughing, they slapped their paddles together.

Taylor tapped Will's paddle with hers a second time, her grin relieved. "No need for second thoughts, huh?"

Captivated by the healthy pink in her cheeks and excited light in her eyes, he grinned back. "Guess n—"

"Steady." Jax's command rose over the increasing roar of water. "Second set's coming."

The raft rocked, then rotated on swift currents that spun the nose back around.

"Forward!" Jax yelled.

Will dug his paddle into the water, flinching as a wave slammed into the raft, lifting one side of it out of the water. Andi tumbled sideways along the raft's floor, her hands scrambling for a renewed hold.

The rapids turned violent, forcing the raft toward a hole on the right.

The roar of water almost drowned out Jax's shout. "To the left! Hard!"

Will dug his paddle back into the current, pushing strongly with the others, trying to correct the raft's course, but the rapids sucked them farther to the right. They raced along the outskirts of the hole, dipped down, then lifted high on a wave, the bottom of the raft aimed straight for a mammoth pile of rocks jutting out from the center of the river.

"Brace!" Jax shouted.

Will's muscles seized as his attention fixated on the back of Andi's helmet, a thin protection against the rocks. "Andi, hold o—"

The raft slammed into hard stone and a wave flipped,

then pinned, it against the rocks, dumping everyone into the river.

Rapid currents pulled Will under. Green mountains and gray sky disappeared and water filled his ears, nose and mouth. He spun uncontrollably to the left. Then a wave swelled and threw him to the right. Lungs burning, he kicked until his feet hit the rocky riverbed. Then he shoved off and swam upward, his head finally breaking the surface.

He spit out a mouthful of water and dragged in a ragged breath. Disoriented, he bobbed along the rising swell of a wave, blinking hard against the spray of water, focusing on clouds, rocks, then water until he spotted the flash of Andi's red helmet several feet downriver.

"Dad!" Her arm flailed in the air before she was sucked underwater.

Will kicked with the roiling rapids, pivoting his body toward Andi as he floated over rough waters downriver. She reappeared on the swell of a wave, stopped near a boulder at a bend in the river, then went back under.

"Swim, An—"

Waves rolled over Will, spun him, then slammed him into the hard boulder. He gripped a rough edge with both hands, heaved his upper body out of the water and glanced over his left shoulder, where Andi struggled two feet away.

Her arms thrashed above the water and the red helmet emerged again. Will reached out with one hand, gripped Andi's forearm and pulled her to the surface, where she gasped for breath.

"Swim to me, Andi," Will shouted, his throat raw. She was a great swimmer, and so close. If he could just pull her closer and get her safely to the boulder— Why couldn't he pull her closer? "Andi, swi—"

"I—I can't!" A series of waves beat at Andi, washing over her face, stealing her breath. Will pulled harder until she reached the surface again, gasping, "My foot's caught. I—"

The current sucked Andi back under, ripping her arm from his grip. He tightened his hold on the rough edge of the boulder and lunged deeper into the water, his hand plunging low, fingers slipping under the shoulder of Andi's life jacket and yanking her back up.

She barely broke the surface this time, coughing and sputtering, still trapped by an undercut rock, now at least three feet away from the boulder. Away from him.

Her eyes, wide and panicked, clung to his face. "Don't let go, Daddy." Blue tinged her trembling lips. "Please don't let me g—"

White water engulfed her again, obscuring the red helmet.

"No!" Will yanked hard, straining to maintain his grip on the boulder as the current dragged Andi farther away, stretching his arm to the point of pain. "Someone help m—"

Waves slapped his face, stinging his eyes. He curled his hand tighter around Andi's life jacket and scanned the raging waters for help. No one was nearby and he couldn't see the raft. He and Andi had drifted downriver, away from the group. There was nothing but white water breaking against thick stone.

"Andi!" Will's arm shook as he struggled to pull Andi back to the surface. How long had she been under this time? Three seconds? Four? Dread seeped into his veins, flooded his chest and spilled onto his cheeks. If he let go of the boulder now, tried to free her and failed, he might lose his hold on her completely and be swept downriver while she'd be left alone to dr—

Please, God, help me. He couldn't let Andi drown. Couldn't watch his baby girl flail beneath the water until…

"Please, God, don't take her from me."

Chapter Two

In the end, there's only us.

Lungs burning, Taylor kicked against the river's current and strained to reach air. Her foot struck a stone on the riverbed, a sharp edge cutting the sole of her waterproof sneaker, digging into her heel.

Do you see this now?

Preston's face appeared behind her tightly closed eyelids: his brown eyes wide and urgent, lean cheeks slicked with sweat and voice oddly calm as it passed sneering lips. Even now, she could feel his blunt thumbnails digging into the base of her throat. For some reason, he'd always attacked her neck first.

"In the end, Taylor," he'd say, staring down, squeezing tighter, "there's only us. Do you see this now?" Tighter. "Do you see?"

Taylor kicked harder, stroked her arms vigorously through the churning water and finally broke the surface. She opened her eyes and dragged in air, her chest swelling in tandem with the wave that moved beneath her, shoving her toward the left side of the river.

Gray sky, white froth and sharp mountain peaks flashed by as waves rolled her supine, jerked her upright and yanked at her limbs. Water burned her nostrils, flooded her ears, filled her mouth. She spit it out and kept her eyes on the sky, focusing on the thunderhead directly above her. The misshapen charcoal-colored mass watched, mute and detached, as the rapids flung her onto her back and thrust her farther downriver.

Maybe... she thought. Maybe Preston had—

Taylor slammed to a stop, her left rib cage hitting a solid wall.

The swirling clouds slowed and the mountains stilled. Her legs stretched out in front of her, the relentless current pulling her feet around a boulder. Taylor rolled over, threw her arms out and scrambled to take hold of the massive rock. She curled her palms around a jagged edge and dug her nails in.

Breath rasping from her shaky lips, she blinked away a fresh spray of water and peered upriver. The raft, pinned upside down against a rock when she'd last seen it, was no longer visible. Jax, who'd been clinging to the raft, reaching for Beth and Martin as they'd struggled in the water, had disappeared from view behind a long, unfamiliar stretch of rough rapids and rocky bends in the river. There didn't seem to be a soul around.

How far had she drifted?

"Andi!"

Taylor started at the desperate cry, recognizing the

deep tone of Will's voice. It rose above the crash of water and echoed against the steep, rocky banks surrounding them, seeming to originate from the other side of the boulder where she'd found refuge.

Carefully, she pulled hard on the boulder, lifted her upper body out of the water and plastered her hips and legs against the rock. Waves beat at her back, but she dragged her knees up, tucked the soles of her feet against the boulder and scaled its face, edging around its rough-hewn corner through the water until the fingers of her right hand bumped Will's.

At her touch, his broad-knuckled grip tightened on the boulder and he looked up. His eyes, intense below the rim of his helmet, locked with hers over the muscles straining in his outstretched arm.

"She can't breathe." His other arm flexed, yanking harder at a life jacket submerged in the roiling white water. A red helmet rose toward the surface, then sank farther below. "Her foot's caught." His lips trembled. "Please help her."

Taylor tentatively gripped his white-knuckled fist on the boulder, testing the solidness of his hold, then inched one hand over his thick wrist and down his flexed forearm. Her stomach dipped at the uneasy feel of heavy male muscle beneath her shaky fingertips, but she inhaled sharply and forced her body closer, following the curve of his upper arm, shoulder, then chest.

Level with him now, she wrapped her palm around the strong dip between his neck and shoulder and called out above the roar of the rapids, "Can you take my weight and still hold on?"

He nodded, the rough stubble lining his clenched jaw brushing her wet cheek.

A heavy wave slammed into her back and she bobbed between the boulder and Will. Clenching her teeth, she let go of the boulder and shifted her weight onto him.

He grunted as she carefully climbed across his body against the fierce barrage of water. The color in his cheeks deepened to a fierce red and tremors ran through his outstretched arms.

Taylor tucked one hand beneath the lower edge of his life jacket, secured her grip, then dropped below the water's tumultuous surface. Cold water engulfed her and the fierce current tangled her long hair over her face and obscured her vision.

She reached out, her fingers groping blindly down Will's submerged arm until a hard, round surface hit her palm. Almost instantly, a hand latched on to her wrist and pulled.

Andi's brown eyes, wild as she thrashed underwater, widened up at Taylor. She stabbed one hand toward the riverbed, pointing at an undercut rock that trapped her foot.

Taylor released Will's life jacket and grabbed Andi's instead. She dived deeper through the raging current until she reached the undercut rock. Probing past the rock's jagged edge with one hand, she grabbed Andi's ankle and pulled. It didn't budge.

Above her, a muted sound escaped Andi as she continued kicking with her free leg. The motion, once fast and frenzied, had weakened, and Andi's eyes began to close.

Taylor released Andi's life jacket, grabbed Andi's ankle with both hands and braced her feet on the riverbed. She pulled Andi's foot to the right, then left, tugging hard, her hopes fading as her lungs screamed for oxygen until—*finally*—it popped free!

Relieved, Taylor shoved off the riverbed and swam up. Her arms strained for the water's surface, but Andi, her energy spurred on by the release, kicked frantically, striking her temple.

Tumultuous water, like vicious hands, snatched her limbs and dragged Taylor away, churning her body through rough waves and slamming her against rocks. She fought her way back to the surface and stole one deep breath before the rapids sucked her under again. Dim, murky light from an unreachable sky melted away and dark depths rolled over her, smothering her burning lungs, clogging her throat. The loud rush of water receded, silence descended and a heavy sensation settled over her weak limbs.

Maybe... Taylor closed her eyes and unfurled her fists. Maybe Preston had been right.

The sharp pull on Will's arm released. He fell back against the boulder, his biceps stinging and his heart faltering painfully until a red helmet burst through the surface of the water.

Andi, openmouthed, sucked in a strong breath.

Will fisted his hand around her life jacket and dragged her in, hauling her onto the rough edge of the boulder. Fingers trembling, he touched her cheeks, shoulders and hands—all blue-tinged and cold, but otherwise sound. "Thank God." He spun back to the river and reached down, but his hand only met the spray of icy water through empty air. "Where's Taylor?"

Andi coughed, her rapid breaths slowing to long drags of air. "I…I kicked her." She stared up at him and her expression crumpled. "She got my foot free. Then I—" A sob escaped her. "I didn't mean to."

Will scanned the river, hoping for a glimpse of her. Maybe she swam to another boulder and managed to pull herself to safety? Or found refuge on the other side of the bank?

Whitecapped waves broke against rocks on the right side of the river, deep water poured over steep inclines on the left and thick trees lining both banks of the river bent with the wind above empty ground. Taylor was nowhere in sight.

"There." Andi's wet arm brushed his jaw as she pointed to the left, her fingertip aligning with the flash of a blue helmet in the distance that floated along a bend in the river. Taylor lifted an arm in the air briefly before she disappeared beneath the surface. "She had nothing to hold on to when I—" Andi's voice broke. She moved toward the water but doubled over, a cry of pain escaping her as she cradled her ankle with both hands. "We can't just leave her."

"I know." Instinctively, Will covered Andi's hands with his own and moved them aside. Deep abrasions and slight swelling marred her smooth skin. Gritting his teeth, he shoved painful thoughts of what might've happened to the back of his mind and focused on Taylor, who reemerged and floated on her back, limbs barely moving, near the bend in the river. She had to be exhausted, and now her safety depended on the mercy of the rapids.

Water moved high and fast, the few rocks leading toward the river's bank were too far apart to be quickly traversed and no one else was nearby. The only chance of reaching Taylor quickly—or at all—was through the water. But plunging back into the rapids would be risky and meant leaving Andi behind…

Will lowered his legs back into the river. No way would he abandon Taylor—especially not when she'd risked her own life to save Andi's. "Stay here."

"I can cross the rocks and make it to the bank, then—"

"You'll stay here." He cupped Andi's chin, tugged her face toward him and met her eyes. "Your ankle the way it is, you got a better chance of falling back in than making it to the bank." His breath caught at the thought, but urgency surged through his veins, pushing him farther into the water. "Wait here. I'll get Taylor, then come back for you."

"But I can help. Let me go with y—"

"*Please*, Andi!" Every second carried Taylor farther away. He dropped lower, cold water rising over his chest. "Just this once, do what I say."

She stared down at him, trepidation flooding her expression. "You'll come back?" Her voice shook. "Promise you'll come back."

Will studied her face, the dimple in her chin, high

cheekbones and wounded expression. All were so reminiscent of Heather at the same age. Chest aching, he forced himself to release her and eased fully into the water. "I promise."

Swift currents yanked him away and he stretched his arms out, leveraging himself against passing rocks to control his direction. Water, whirling violently along a slight drop, sucked him under, then thrust him back to the surface. He inhaled, rubbed his wet eyes and glanced over his shoulder.

Andi stared back at him. Expression worried, she shifted to her hands and knees and crawled across the boulder toward the string of large rocks leading to the left bank of the river.

"Don't, Andi!"

Roaring rapids drowned out Will's shout, and her small figure, crouched on the boulder, right arm stretching out, hand touching a neighboring rock, disappeared around the bend in the river.

Nice. He grimaced, though he had to admit Andi's actions were unsurprising. For the past two years, she hadn't listened to a word he'd said. Why should now be any different?

Biting back his fear, he peered up at a small sliver of sunlight that barely cut through the gray storm clouds gathering overhead. *You wanna help me out, God?* His chin trembled. *Maybe get Andi safely across the rocks to the bank? Please?*

A soft drizzle began, rain coating his cheeks, mingling with the rapids' misty spray. Mountains, on both sides of him, loomed taller, impeding his view of the sky, as the river shoved him over a long succession of rocky drops. Rocks, trees and increasingly dark clouds swept past, each stretch of rapids dragging him farther away from Andi, seeming to go on forever.

Will forced his tight muscles to relax and surrendered his body, feetfirst, to the current, following its swift pull, gaining ground. Water sprayed his face, stinging his eyes, but he managed to keep his head up, eyes focused ahead.

And there—several feet ahead to the right—floated Taylor, her body traveling along a smooth stretch of water that flowed toward a thick log protruding from the bank. Beyond this, the rapids converged and disappeared over a steep waterfall, a merciless crash of water echoing in the distance.

His muscles seized. "Taylor!"

She gave no response, and the slow tread of her arms and legs had stopped. The current continued to carry her.

Will shifted his weight to the side, pushed off a passing rock with his feet and swam along a swelling wave in Taylor's direction. He kicked hard with the current and grabbed at her hand, floating limply on the water's surface, but missed.

The log—his only chance of anchoring himself and Taylor to the bank before reaching the falls—drew closer. Lunging, he made one last, desperate grab and latched on to her wrist.

Will drew her in, tucked his hand beneath the shoulder of her life jacket and flung his free arm toward the log...only to watch in dismay as the current spun him away, forcing him and Taylor to the edge of the waterfall.

He wrapped his arms around Taylor's limp, unconscious form. Pictured Andi, stranded miles away. "Please, God—"

For a moment, the river's bank tilted, laid on its side, then fell away. Will's gut hollowed as they plunged over the steep falls.

A swift burst of racing water and wind mixed, slicing over and around them, diving between his and Taylor's tangled limbs, then spit them out, tumbling them into a new set of raging rapids at the base of the waterfall.

Will broke the water's surface, inhaled deeply and threw his free arm out. His hand hit a large rock, gripped a jagged edge, then pulled. Holding Taylor tight to his side, he dragged them both out of the sucking current, then carried Taylor across two large rocks until he hit hard ground.

Falling to his knees, he focused on an exposed root of a cedar tree until his dizziness subsided, then gently laid her down. He removed Taylor's helmet and eased her head to the side.

Water drained from her parted lips. He brought her face back to his, covered her mouth with his own and delivered five strong breaths. Compressions were next.

Hands fumbling, he removed her life jacket, pressed his palms to the center of her chest and pumped firmly. The feel of soft flesh and fragile bone beneath the frantic press of his hands froze his movements.

Too much pressure or not enough? What if he did

more damage than good? And if this didn't work, was there anything else that would?

"Taylor?" He leaned close, brought his ear level with her mouth, but couldn't hear or feel her pull in a breath.

Tilting her head back, he provided more oxygen. "Come on, Taylor. Help me out. Breathe."

He pressed his fingertips to the delicate skin below her jaw, feeling for a pulse.

A ragged sound left her lips. Her chest lifted on a strong inhalation and her eyes opened.

Will sagged with relief. "'Bout time." He forced a shaky smile. "For a second, I thought—"

Her hand struck his wrist, dislodging his touch from her neck. She scrambled backward, but barely moved, her weakened legs struggling to push against the sandy bank beneath her and her shaky arms failing to drag her exhausted body away. Ragged coughs racked her frame, but her eyes remained pinned to his face. Terror darkened the blue depths.

"Easy..." He looked down at her and held his hand up slowly, palm out. "You were in the water a long time. Almost drowned."

She clutched her neck, her fingers covering the small area he'd touched below her jaw. "Ba—" Voice breaking, she dragged air in between shaky, blue-tinged lips, then tried again. "Back off."

"I didn't mean to scare you. I was just—"

"I said, back off."

He studied the fear and accusation moving through her expression, noted the shade of bright pink that bloomed across her pale cheeks, then slowly rose and walked to the river's edge.

Will tried to shove his hands in his pockets, but the soggy cloth clung to his palms. He'd never revived someone before. Hadn't been sure what to expect. But it certainly hadn't been this. He understood her fear: she'd almost drowned, he was little more than a stranger to her and the rapids had put them both through the wringer. But still…

"I wasn't trying to hurt you," he said softly. "You saved my daughter's life. I wasn't going to stand by while you struggled."

He glanced back at her. Taylor still cradled her neck with one hand and the other lifted to her face, her fingertips trembling as they touched her lips. She looked so vulnerable, so lost.

Will jerked back around and eyed the steep waterfall several feet upriver. Violent water poured in erratic patterns over rough rocks and knotty roots. The falls had plunged them into a gorge, and there was no way out but up the one-hundred-foot wall beside the falls.

He peered beyond the sharp incline toward the dark clouds. Light rain still fell and he blinked against it, flinching as a low rumble of thunder rolled in the distance. It originated upriver, where Andi—injured and alone—still waited for him. Only now, she may be tumbling down the same watery path he and Taylor had traveled, or she could still be dragging herself across the rocks, trying to reach the bank—the bank opposite the one on which he stood.

Either way, more than a raging river separated them.

A storm brewed, daylight faded and miles of unfamiliar terrain lay ahead. And who knew what dangers would creep through the darkness to where Andi sought refuge for the night? That was if she made it out of the river and could find decent shelter from the storm.

He should never have brought Andi out here.

"We're even."

The steel in Taylor's tone surprised Will. She stared back at him, eyes wary.

"Like you said." Taylor sat upright, pulled her knees to her chest and wrapped her arms around her shins. "I helped Andi, and now you've helped me. I can take care of myself from here on out. So that makes us even."

"No," he bit out. "It doesn't." His throat tightened, making it difficult to speak, but a dark restless hollow inside him kept spewing words. "My daughter's hurt. Stranded miles upriver on the other side of the waterfall, waiting on me to make good on my promise and come back for her. A storm's moving in, the rapids are impassable here and it'll take me an hour—or more—to scale that wall without equipment. There's no way I can make that climb tonight."

Will stifled a groan and closed his eyes. What if Andi hadn't made it to the bank? What if she'd given up and sat exposed, right now, on the boulder where he'd left her, shivering as the storm approached?

No. Whatever might've happened, Andi would've kept going. Matter of fact, if he was a betting man, he'd wager his last dime that was exactly what she was doing right now. Soon as the rain started sprinkling down on her, as headstrong as she was, Andi would've moved even faster across those rocks, dragging her injured ankle behind her. And she'd be at the mercy of whatever lay beyond the thick trees lining the riverbank.

They don't call this river Bear's Tooth for nothing...

Will's throat closed as he recalled Jax's words. The waterfall blurred, melting into the rain-drenched wooded terrain surrounding it.

"I'm sorry," Taylor said quietly. Her face flushed a deep shade of red. "I didn't mean to—"

"To what?" He clenched his fists. "If not for you and Jax—" *and me* "—agreeing to continue, Andi would—"

Lightning shot above them, streaking over the waterfall like a dozen spindly legs, and a vicious crack of thunder rattled the ground beneath his feet.

Will grabbed both life jackets and helmets. "Can you walk?"

Taylor pried her attention away from the waterfall and blinked up at him. "What?"

"Are you able to stand—" he stabbed a hand toward the rocky base of the waterfall "—and hike back that way? There might be a dry place below one of those outcrops where we can wait out the storm."

Taylor nodded jerkily. "Yes." She stood slowly, her legs visibly trembling. The movements cost her. Pain showed in the tight press of her lips and flinch of her shoulders, but she straightened and met his eyes. "I'm sorry. I never meant to put Andi in danger."

She meant every word. Regret was right there in her voice, in her eyes, in the slight quiver of her dimpled chin. And it wasn't her fault. The decision to bring Andi to the river this morning had been his alone, and nothing could undo that now.

Will caught himself reaching for Taylor, the urge to console her and seek reassurance for his own misguided intentions almost overwhelming. But neither of those actions would erase the guilt gnawing at his gut or lead him to Andi any faster. Instead, he walked away.

Chapter Three

She should've thanked him. Should've realized Will was trying to help her, rather than have mistaken his pain for anger.

Taylor frowned and forced one heavy foot in front of the other, her lungs aching and muscles shaking as she hiked toward the waterfall. Shoulda, coulda, woulda, right? Too late to fix it now. Or was it?

Will, leading the way to the falls, paused a few steps ahead and glanced back at her. "You good?"

She squinted against the fat raindrops hitting her cheeks, but couldn't make out his expression. Night had fallen, rain had intensified and the blinding pulse of light preceding each roll of thunder proved the storm had settled right on top of them for the foreseeable future.

"Yeah," she called out. "I'm okay."

Though she was certain he already knew that. He'd maintained his stiff posture and heavy tread over the half mile they'd hiked so far, but every six feet, he'd slowed his pace and glanced over his shoulder to make sure she still followed. The slight downward tilt of his head hinted he was giving her a once-over, and satisfied she still stood upright, he'd faced forward and resumed hiking.

"We're almost there." Lightning poured over the sky and flooded the riverbank, briefly bringing his sculpted cheekbones and chiseled jawline into sharp relief. "There's an opening to the right of the falls just ahead. Might be a decent place to get out of this."

Even now, after Will had selflessly dragged her from the river and breathed air into her lungs, Taylor stiffened in his presence. Stranded alone in this rough backcountry, being pummeled by the violent throb of the storm surrounding them, would've been enough to raise her guard. But each blinding flash of lightning illuminated his impressive height and muscular girth, heightening her apprehension. It was clear he blamed her for their current predicament and for endangering his daughter.

Though she should be used to shouldering blame. Her marriage to Preston had been filled with accusations and recriminations. But she used to believe that no matter how strong Preston had been, if she kept her spirit stronger, he couldn't break her. No matter how much he'd blamed her for his attacks, no matter how tightly he'd clenched his hands around her throat or how sharply his heel had hammered her ribs, if she'd just held on to that sliver of hope that still pulsed inside her and prayed, something would change. God would deliver some form of relief, and eventually she'd escape whole. When she'd finally found the courage to pick herself up, leave him and find a place of her own, she thought she had.

But Preston had proved her wrong.

"Taylor?" Will, now still, studied her closely. His eyes narrowed beneath the steady rivulets of water streaming over his brow and his expression softened as he lowered their life jackets and helmets toward the ground. "Do you need me to help y—?"

"No." The word left her lips sharper than she'd intended. She squeezed her eyes shut, then focused on the steep waterfall ahead. "Keep going. Sooner we get there, sooner we're out of this."

Heavy wind tore through the tree line and shoved at their backs, driving her point home. Will nodded, hitched the life jackets and helmets back into his arms and pressed on.

She followed, stumbling twice over piles of sharp rocks, until the waterfall's steady roar cut through the chaotic thunder booming above them.

Will pointed to a stretch of dry rock wall below an outcrop. "Wait here. I'm gonna slip inside that opening and take a look."

Taylor ducked beneath the outcrop and pressed against the wall. Sharp rocky edges dug into her back, but they were solid and supportive, prompting her to sag against them. Every muscle in her body screamed beneath her skin and she rolled her head to the right, peering into the space Will had entered.

Inside, the small cave was black and shapeless, but each flash of lightning lit up the space, revealing a smooth, rocky floor, uneven walls and a high interior ceiling. Will's large frame moved slowly and carefully. His long legs took small steps and his strong arms reached out, palms testing the sturdiness of each wall.

"It's safe." His deep voice drew closer as he approached her. His brown eyes, intense, skimmed her trembling length. "Can you make it in on your own?"

Her limbs balked at the thought of moving, but she nodded, slowly pushed off the wall and trudged inside. The sound of the pounding rain receded as dry walls enveloped them in a stone cocoon.

"We passed some deadfall outside," Will said.

It was dark for a moment, the relentless lightning having briefly stilled. The disembodied timbre of his voice sounded strangely comforting.

"Some of the wood is sheltered by the outcrop," he continued. "It should be dry enough to burn with a bit of elbow grease. It won't take me long to round it up."

Shivering, Taylor sat on the dry stone floor and drew her knees to her chest. "Okay."

Lightning relit the cave on Will's departure and she was alone. Minutes—which felt more like hours—passed, her raspy breaths echoing against the walls, hitching each time blustery wind cracked tree limbs and the shallow walls of the cave groaned. She lifted her hand to her chest, touching her tender sternum where she assumed Will's hands had forced water from her lungs. Her clothes were wet and the swimsuit she wore beneath them clung to her clammy skin, sending a chill through her.

Will returned, his arms filled with thin twigs, sturdy

sticks and a handful of dry moss. His heavy footsteps echoed in the small space as he drew near her side, dumped the stack of wood on the stone floor and knelt beside her.

"Hopefully, there's enough dry wood here to build a fire and get us through the next few hours. From what I could tell, none of our supplies floated downriver with us." There were scuffling noises as he shifted his weight and dug around for something in his pockets. "No telling where our dry bags are by now—we can look for those in the morning—but luckily, one tool traveled with us."

He held up a small item and lightning flashed, reflecting off the sharp edge of a knife before darkness settled over them again. Taylor stiffened.

"This is one time I'm glad I forgot to pack something," Will continued. "Jax borrowed my knife this morning to cut a throw line, and I never got around to putting it back in the dry bag."

He put the knife down, stood, then walked around the cave. Stones clinked in different directions. Then he returned and dumped several large rocks onto the floor beside the knife.

The storm raged on, rain pummeling their crude shelter, as Will worked to build a fire. He broke a thick branch in half with his foot, carved a groove down the center of one half and shaped a point at the end of a smaller stick.

He stopped abruptly, dragged a broad palm over his face and kneaded the back of his neck, his huddled form a dark outline against the backdrop of lightning.

"Here," Taylor said, reaching out. "I'll get the fire started while you catch your breath."

He stilled. Then his hand fumbled over hers, tucking the pointed stick into her grasp.

She felt her way around the pile of dry wood, using the rhythmic bursts of lightning to guide her movements as she strategically stacked the dry wood, used the rocks Will had gathered to form a fire ring, then built a fire. It'd been a while and she struggled, but finally found success, then sagged back onto her knees and watched the flames grow.

One corner of Will's mouth lifted in a wry grin. "Thanks for that. Hate to admit when I'm beat, but that river stole the last of my reserves for the day."

She nodded. "From all of us, I think. Everyone is probably exhausted by now." A spider escaped the woodpile and scurried away from the hot flames. "Wherever they are."

Will's grin faded and his gaze drifted toward the rain whipping sideways outside the cave's entrance. Jaw clenching, he stared at it silently.

"Was Andi okay?" Taylor asked. "When she came out of the water?"

"Her ankle was sprained, but not broken, as far as I could tell. Other than that, she was as hardheaded as she's ever been." Will closed his eyes and rubbed his thumb and forefinger against his eyelids. "Even if she—or the others—made it to the bank, they won't be able to make any calls. There's no cell service out here. It'll take at least two days or more for them to hike back to the drop point and send help."

Firelight danced over his lean cheeks. Taylor studied the tight press of his mouth. "Do you know if anyone else is planning to run the river this week?"

"No." He opened his eyes and stared at the fire. "There's always a chance, but..." He shoved to his feet, jerked the hem of his wet T-shirt up to his midriff, then froze, his dark eyes meeting hers. "I'm soaked. My shirt'll dry faster if I spread it by the fire. Do you mind if I take it off?"

She looked away from his toned abs and focused on her hands. "No."

Thick smoke filled her nostrils and the fire's flickering flames cast an eerie red glow, almost like blood, across her exposed palms. Her fingers shook and a tight knot formed in her chest as memories assailed her, dragging her back to a moment five years ago that she'd never been able to fully leave behind.

"What have you done?" Preston hadn't moved at all that morning when she'd dropped the gun, covered the gaping wound in his gut with her hands and pressed hard. Blood had seeped between her spread fingers while she'd pleaded with him to hang on. He'd stared up at her from his supine position on the kitchen floor of the small house she'd rented, shock and anger in his dilating eyes, his voice fading as he'd continued. *"You can't fix it now."*

Shivering, Taylor twisted her hands together and rubbed her wet palms hard.

Will cleared his throat, his voice hesitant. "I don't mean to make you uncomfortable, but Andi wears a suit under her clothes when we hit the river. She's probably cold to the bone right now." His words weakened on a saddened tone. "Anyway, I've got my back turned. If you've got a suit on and want to dry it out, you have the privacy to do it. You've got my word."

Taylor touched her wet T-shirt absently, then glanced at Will, whose back was—true to his word—facing her. Firelight and shadow played over his muscular stature.

"I—I'll take you up on that," she said. "Thank you."

His dark head dipped and he maintained his position.

Quickly, she slipped her hands under her T-shirt, peeled her swimsuit off her shoulders, arms and down her waist, then stood and tugged off her shorts long enough to remove the suit. She redonned her shorts and shirt, spread her suit out by the fire and crossed her arms over her chest.

"Okay," she said. "I'm done now."

Will returned to his seat beside the fire. He kept his eyes averted as he held his hands out, warming them by the flames. "You built a good fire. We'll be dry soon." He glanced at her, then quickly looked away. "I imagine you're exhausted. I promise you're safe with me. I'll keep an eye on things if you want to lie down and get some sleep."

She scanned the floor. "I'm not too keen on that, but it's not so much you I'm worried about right now. I've seen at least three spiders crawling around. I'm not anxious to stretch out beside them or lean against a wall they may be nesting on."

A low laugh escaped him. "After all we've been up against today, spiders are what's worrying you?"

His smile, for a brief moment, brightened his expression and obscured the shadows in his eyes.

She managed to smile back. “Guess so.”

He glanced around, rolled his lips together as he thought, then slid closer and presented his back to her again. “Lean back against me. If we do this right, you can sleep sitting up.”

Taylor hesitated as she studied the strong curves of his exposed back. His bare upper body, relaxed by the fire, seemed much less intimidating. Which was worse? Taking a chance on a half-naked stranger, or risk being bitten by a black widow?

“Taylor?” His voice, softening, barely rose above a roll of thunder. He eyed her over his shoulder. “I know it’s easy for me to say and much harder for you to believe, but I promise you, you got nothing to fear from me.”

She waited, weighing her options, but fatigue won out. Sighing, she slid around and scooted closer until her back met his. Immediately, his dry solid warmth cut through her soggy T-shirt and heat bloomed across her chilled skin. Her muscles relaxed, her body sagged against his supportive weight and, soon, the sporadic crackle of the fire made her eyes heavy.

“Do you pray?” Will’s deep tone filled the empty cave.

Blinking slowly, Taylor turned her head to stare at the fire. “I used to.” Still did, at times.

“Will you pray for my daughter?” Will asked. The deep, worried throb of his voice vibrated against her back, beckoning her to press closer, to plant her hands on the floor, her elbows touching his. "That she stays safe until I find her?"

Words formed in Taylor's mind, her lips moving silently in prayer out of habit before stilling. For a moment, she watched flames lick the dark walls surrounding them, then asked, "Does He answer you?"

Will's back flexed as he turned his head, his soft breath brushing her left ear. "Sometimes."

"But not every time?"

He shook his head. "No. Well…maybe. Sometimes I think He answers, just not in the way I expect. Not in a way I'm looking for. So maybe those times, I'm not able to hear Him."

"Maybe," she repeated. But maybe those times, He didn't answer at all.

"I've lived without Him," Will continued quietly. "And I've lived with Him. The latter is by far the better. At least for me. I keep talking to Him, and He comes through one way or another. Whether I hear Him or not, I believe He always pulls me through the rough times." His tone firmed. "Always."

Taylor closed her eyes, watched the muted orange glow of the fire behind her eyelids and whispered, "Then why let it happen at all?"

"What?"

"The rough times. Andi, stranded on her own." The center of her chest throbbed. "The awful things we do to each other." She pressed her hands together, the memory of blood on her palms almost tangible. "Why does He let it happen at all?"

Will tensed, and she could feel him searching for words.

Taylor pressed closer to him, tilted her head and waited. Strained to hear his voice, a reassurance of some kind. But smoke continued to fill the dark cave. Outside, the storm raged on. And an answer never came.

Birds chattered, water rushed in the distance and something firm and slightly uncomfortable poked Will's temple. He opened his eyes and gradually focused on a thin ray of light inching across the rocky ceiling above him.

Andi.

He sat upright, his quads and abs smarting at the abrupt movement, and looked around. A life jacket lay on the floor behind him, the small impression where his head had rested still visible. The fire had died, leaving only black ash and charred wood behind, and Taylor—along with her swimsuit—was gone.

Will stood, grabbed his dry T-shirt and tugged it on as he walked out of the cave. Fresh, clean air rushed into his lungs and cool mist eased over his bare skin. The storm had moved on, leaving wispy clouds scattered across a slowly brightening sky. Sunlight pooled behind a dense cloak of fog, the sun struggling to burn through as it rose between two mountain peaks.

Taylor stood on the bank of the river, her shapely silhouette, in its stillness, a stark contrast to the violent river, smoky fog and faint streaks of lavender and pink above the mountain peaks. Her head was tilted back, her face lifted toward the high, rocky bank that walled in the waterfall. White water roared over the waterfall and plunged into swollen rapids below, crashing against sharp rocks.

An uneasy ache spread through Will as his gaze followed hers, studying the tangle of green rocks, small bushes and winding vines. Somewhere on the other side of that imposing wall, miles away, Andi, injured and afraid, had spent hours alone in the dark wilderness.

Why does He let it happen at all?

Taylor's question had stayed with Will last night long after she'd fallen asleep, and it had tugged at his subconscious even as he'd slept—rising to the forefront of his mind and tangling with his fitful dreams. It had only receded when he'd opened his eyes, focused on the pulse of lightning outside the cave and forced himself to recall the few things that had gone right that day: Andi, from what he'd been able to gauge, hadn't broken a bone during the overturning of the raft, Taylor had managed to save Andi from drowning when it had seemed there was nothing more that could be done and, even after plunging back into the water and leaving himself at the mercy of the river—a reckless choice but the only viable one available at the time—he'd pulled Taylor to the bank and they'd managed to find shelter from the storm.

He could've easily overlooked all of those blessings—very easily. Still could, if he didn't keep his eyes and heart open.

Taylor's heart seemed firmly closed. The terror in her eyes yesterday on the riverbank as he'd looked down at her had to be a result of more than the day's events, and the despair underlying her question last night in the cave hadn't escaped his notice. But what had caused it? And why, with Andi stranded alone miles away, did he feel a longing to stay close to Taylor's side? To find a crack in her armor and reach the softer, wounded side she'd offered a glimpse of last night when she'd asked her quiet question?

Will left the mouth of the cave and made his way down the soggy bank, his shoes surprisingly sturdy across the muddy ground. A soft breeze rattled the tall trees, shook the branches above him and dropped residual raindrops onto his bare arms. Despite the growl of his empty gut and cotton-like feel of his tongue, the high mountain peaks and steady flow of the river sparked a renewed sense of energy in his muscles and quickened his step.

He lifted a silent prayer of thanks for waking refreshed despite his disturbed sleep. But even though his body physically seemed ready to tackle the formidable barrier of rock, a sense of uncertainty roiled within him. Andi, wherever she was, had probably not had the benefit of a sheltering cave last night, and she definitely hadn't had someone with her to share the fear and shock of the day's painful events during the stormy hours until sunrise. Every bit of his focus should be on reaching Andi as soon as possible and nothing—or no one—else.

Will reached Taylor's side, studied her profile, then spoke. "It won't be easy, but it's doable."

A blond curl lifted in the morning breeze, danced

across her freckled cheek, then rested on her lips. She tucked it behind her ear and nodded. “It’s steep, mostly limestone with several big holds. But there’s a lot of vegetation and probably loose rocks hidden along the crevices.” Sunlight glowed behind the fog hovering above them and cast a golden hue over her face and neck. She turned her head, her blue eyes locking with his. “What’s your guess on the height?”

Will shoved his hands in his pockets as he focused on the rock wall. “Hundred, hundred and ten feet. A bit more, maybe? But at those numbers, the exact measurement doesn’t really matter, does it?”

“No.” Her confident tone faded. “Halfway up, one slip, one fall, it’s over.” She drew in a strong breath and pointed at the river. “I searched every inch of the bank I could reach this morning, and none of our dry bags made it over the falls. All our equipment is either pinned beneath the raft or hung up on rocks upriver. We’ve got no harnesses, rope or chalk. And so far as I know, no one’s ever scaled this wall. We won’t have any anchors to use as a guide.”

Will narrowed his eyes. “We?”

A determined expression crossed her face. “Yes.”

“Look—” he held up a hand “—I know I put a lot of the blame for what happened on you, and I’m sorry for that. Last night, I was angry and afraid for Andi. But you’re no more responsible for our predicament than me.” He swallowed hard, choking back a surge of guilt and fear. “I’m the one who brought Andi out here, and as her dad, I’m responsible for finding her. You’re under no obligation to climb those rocks or scour these mountains for her. There's no reason you can't stay here, safe on the ground."

"There's one reason," Taylor said softly. She studied his face. "I like Andi. She's got spirit and drive. And you saved my life yesterday. Something I don't think I properly thanked you for." Her gaze shifted. Drifted to a point over his left shoulder. "You seem like a good man, and considering the circumstances, you could probably use some help. I'm not offering because I feel like I have to. I'm offering because I want to."

He shouldn't accept. Climbing that wall would be dangerous, and there was no telling what threats lurked beyond it. He should turn her down gently, embark on the journey alone and find a modicum of comfort in the fact that she remained somewhere relatively safe.

But the supportive feel of her leaning into him last night in the cave still lingered with him this morning, and the thought of scaling the wall and hiking terrain with someone by his side rather than on his own was too tempting to refuse. Her willingness to risk her life again—in spite of the doubts she'd expressed hours earlier in the cave—for Andi…well, he couldn't help but admire the strength in that choice.

"Have you climbed walls like this before?" he asked.

"Yeah. Routinely." She faced the waterfall again, her eyes tracing the water's path as it poured over the rock wall, plunged into the rapids and broke among submerged rocks. "But I've never free soloed before. It's a whole nother game climbing an unfamiliar route alone without equipment."

"We've got one thing in our favor." Will tilted his head back and watched as a ray of sunlight pierced the fog above them. "If we climb together, neither one of us will be alone."

Chapter Four

Taylor leaned forward on the riverbank, dug her heel into the mud and straightened her back leg, stretching her right calf muscle. The tight pull in her leg gradually subsided, giving way to warm flexible strength, but that small release did nothing to still the unsettling fear roiling within her, and the roar of the waterfall to the left of her only enhanced her anxiety. She'd barely been able to take her eyes off the massive falls during the ten minutes she and Will stretched on the riverbank in preparation for the impending climb.

"Trust," Will said, holding out a helmet.

Straightening, she raised her eyebrows and searched his expression.

"Free-climbing that wall isn't just about physical strength." He lifted the helmet higher and gestured toward her head with his free hand. "May I?"

She eyed the relaxed position of his muscular arm and long fingers, then slowly nodded. "Please."

He moved closer and eased the helmet onto her head.

"A lot of what's needed during the climb is here." His thumb touched the center of her forehead gently before his big hands lowered and fastened the helmet's strap beneath her chin. "The rest—" he pressed his wide palm to the left side of his chest "—is here."

The warmth of his touch lingered on her forehead and bloomed over her cheeks. Fingers trembling, she reached up and checked the chin strap.

"Does it feel secure?" he asked.

"Yes."

She glanced at the waterfall, its majestic height, powerful water and rugged strength almost mesmerizing. The sun had fully risen over the mountain peaks and burned off most of the thick fog above them, flooding the waterfall and narrow gorge with golden hues of light. Water sparkled in every direction.

"Despite the dangers," she said softly, "it is a beautiful sight."

"Shame your camera didn't make it down the river with us." Will put on his helmet and secured his chin strap. "Like you said yesterday, one decent pic of these falls would make the cover of any magazine. Probably fetch a pretty payday, too."

"Probably." Taylor stretched her arms overhead, her muscles trembling. "I just hate that we found it the way we did."

The hesitant look of admiration forming on Will's face melted away as he examined the steep wall in front of them. "It's no wonder why no one's ventured this far downriver before. The only way out of here is up. There are plenty of ledges, so it won't be all wall, but the parts that are just rock will be challenging." He faced her unexpectedly, his somber gaze searching her expression. "Are you afraid?"

A lie hovered on the tip of her tongue. It was so tempting to return his stare, lift her chin and shrug off his concern for the sake of holding this charismatic stranger at a distance. She'd made the mistake of blindly trusting a man once before and it wasn't wise to do it again—especially in these remote, treacherous surroundings. The safer bet would be to put on a brave face and hope he didn't see beyond it. But something in his direct scrutiny hinted he already knew she was second-guessing herself, and the patient kindness he'd shown her over the past hours made her long to lean on him more than she should.

"Yes," she admitted quietly, lowering her arms to her sides. "I'm afraid of just about everything lately."

His expression gentled as he scanned her trembling frame. "If you'd like to lead, I'll climb close behind and promise to do everything I can to support you. Do you trust me enough to try that?"

Trust. One small word rife with so much risk. Taylor fiddled with the hem of her shorts, then forced herself to nod despite the painful kick of her heart against her ribs.

Will smiled. A warm gleam of affection entered his brown eyes, enhancing his handsome features. He held out his hand, palm tilted up in invitation. "Ready?"

Hesitating, she slid her hand in his. The warm strength of his fingers curled around hers and eased some of the nervous tension clamoring through her. "Ready."

They walked to the wall together, hands clasped, until they reached the base of the waterfall. A misty spray of water wet Taylor's cheek and she wiped it away with her free hand.

"Here." Will tugged her farther to the right, away from the spray of the waterfall to a sunlit stretch of rugged wall. "Dry hands make for a better grip." He cradled both of her hands in one of his and proceeded to rub her palms dry with the hem of his T-shirt. "Remember to feel your way up as much as see it. These falls are like a living entity—they move, breathe. And there'll still be damp places from the rain on the fragile parts of the outer walls. Those spots can crack or break if you're not careful." Pausing, he drifted his thumb gently over the tender skin of her wrist. "You don't have to do this, you know? It's not too late to change your mind and keep your feet on the ground."

"No." Taylor squeezed his hands and smiled tightly. "Andi's waiting, and the more help you have, the faster you'll find her." She slipped past him and eyed the rocky ledges, dense vegetation and smooth stones stretching up toward the sky. "We could follow the largest ledges up the right side, then pivot to the outcrop on the left. What do you think?"

Will nodded slowly, his eyes tracing the path she'd pointed out. "Looks like the safest and straightest line to me. You still want to lead?"

"Yes."

He motioned toward the base of the wall. "Take your time. I'll be right behind you."

Taylor inhaled, grabbed on to a low ledge with both hands and hauled her lower body onto the wall. The rough feel of rock beneath her fingers and press of uneven stone into her heels made her pause.

Oh, boy. What had she gotten herself into? It was one thing to imagine scaling over a hundred feet of slippery mountain wall, but it was quite another to leave the ground and cling to rocks in midair.

"Breathe," Will said softly from below. "Keep your eyes up and focus on one hold at a time."

In spite of it all, Taylor grinned. Though his words were kind and patient, he wasn't quite as confident as he seemed. There was a slight hitch in his voice. Not much, but just enough to let her know she wasn't the only one harboring fears of missing a hold, losing her footing, plummeting a hundred feet and breaking against the rocks below.

"You lilted." Still grinning, she reached up, grabbed a smooth edge and hauled her body two feet higher up the wall.

"I what?"

"Lilted." She lifted her left foot to a higher ledge, tested its stability, then, satisfied with its support, climbed higher. "Your tone pitched on your last syllable. I noticed you did it twice last night, too. Once on the riverbank and once in the cave." Another ledge, another three feet higher. "I'm guessing you're as nervous about this climb as I am and don't want to tell me."

A breeze rustled the lush green vegetation that grew

at awkward angles from cracks in the wall. Taylor carefully plucked a damp clump of moss out of a large crevice and probed with her fingers for a safe hold.

"I didn't lilt."

Taylor grinned wider. If she wasn't mistaken, Will's voice had deepened at least an octave. And anything that released a bit of the tension was welcome right now—even a good-natured argument.

"Yeah, you did," she said. "There's no shame in it. I just thought you should know I'd picked up on it and it's kind of comforting." She rested for a moment, breathing deeply as she pressed against the wall. "Not that I'm glad you're uncomfortable. I suppose it's just nice to know I'm not alone in being concerned about making it to the top of this wall." She slowly glanced over her shoulder and peered down at him. "Are you coming or are you just gonna leave me hanging here?"

A slow smile spread across his handsome face. "Glad I could entertain." He grabbed the lowest ledge, hefted himself onto the wall and traced the path she'd traveled, ascending with grace and purpose. When he drew within arm's length, he tapped her ankle gently. "Let's take our time with the next hold," he said in a more relaxed tone. "We can't risk taking a route we can't reverse out of, if needed."

"Okay." Taylor faced the wall again, her stomach dipping.

She didn't know what unsettled her more: the fact that she clung to a hundred-foot wall without rope or a harness, or the knowledge that the only person standing between her and a potentially deadly fall was a charismatic man she'd only known for forty-eight hours and had agreed to trust just minutes ago.

Her attention drifted toward the water cascading over the rock wall several feet away, her eyes clinging to the repeated crash of white water against the boulders below.

"Taylor." Will's calm, focused gaze connected with hers. "Look up. That's where we're headed."

Maybe it was the confident tone of his voice. Or maybe it was the sight of him, strong and capable, planted firmly on the stone ledge below her. Either way, she did as he directed—tore her eyes away from the boulders below and pinned her gaze on the rock wall above her.

For over an hour, they moved slowly and methodically, right arm lifting first, left leg following, then left arm and right leg. Up and up they climbed, the distance between their feet and the bank below lengthening with nerve-racking intensity on each successful series of ascensions. The sun rose higher and blazed hotter, drying limestone and rock and warming stones beneath their fingertips until they almost burned to the touch.

Taylor ran her left hand over a smooth ledge above her, cringing as the scraped skin of her fingertips snagged on the rough rock. Heat from the sun-warmed stone intensified the painful pulse in her hand and blood oozed from a cut on her thumb.

She renewed her grip and pulled, lifting her sweat-slicked brow just above the ledge, and an exhausted laugh burst from her dry lips. "We're almost there! I can see the top. It's only four feet away." Tilting her head to the side, she stared at the summit, too afraid to glance over her shoulder and look down at Will. "Once we make it past this ledge, we're there."

Wind whistled, the chirps of birds peppered the air and Taylor stiffened against the rocks, straining to hear Will's voice.

"That makes you my new best friend." His warm, lighthearted tone and soothing voice was a balm to her trembling muscles. "Ain't gonna lie—" two heavy exhalations sounded below her "—I've been hoping to hear that for a while now."

Taylor smiled but halted the movement, flinching as her chapped lips cracked and a stinging sensation burrowed deep into her gums. She licked her lower lip carefully, then said, "I'm with you. Let's get this over with."

One strong inhalation and one heavy tug and her upper body cleared the ledge. She bent at the waist, lowered her cheek to the smooth stone and rested her arms for a moment, flexing her fingers against the heated rock.

Her tender biceps almost sighed with relief. Only one more heave and haul and she'd reach the summit. She closed her eyes and breathed deeply. Dry dust billowed up, coating her face. Something rustled to her left and a soft rattling sound filled the air.

Taylor froze and opened her eyes slowly.

Three feet away, level with her face, two black eyes glared back at her from a triangular head. The coiled brown body expanded, the black markings along its five-foot length swelled to twice their size and the tip of its tail lifted in the air, a sharp rattle assaulting her ears.

"Taylor?" Will placed his left foot on a narrow jut of rock, gingerly pressed down to test its stability, then, confident it would hold, planted his foot and lifted himself a foot closer to her. "I know you're tired, but this isn't the best place to rest." He dredged up the little bit of humor he had left and tried for a lighthearted tone. "The only thing standing between us and a nice, sturdy place to collapse is one more four-foot climb."

No response.

He studied the stiff set of her legs, noted the tight clench of her calf muscles and frozen position of her feet on the rocks supporting her. The upper half of her body, bent over onto the ledge above him, wasn't visible. "Taylor?" He frowned. "What's going on up there?"

For a moment, the rush of water over the falls and the steady breeze swirling between them and flapping their shorts against their bare thighs were the only sounds. Then Taylor's voice, a mere thread of a whisper that barely carried across the distance between them, emerged.

"Snake."

A bead of sweat stung Will's eye and he winced, blinking it away. "What'd you say?"

"Th-there's a snake." Her voice shook, panic lacing her tone. "About three feet to my left. Coiled on the ledge."

His chest tightened. "All right. Don't pani—"

"Will?"

"Yeah?"

"It's looking at me." Her voice pitched higher. "And it's angry."

He blew out a slow breath. "Okay. Don't panic. Just stay still."

"I am," she whispered loudly. "But I can't stay like this forever."

"I know. What color is it?"

"B-brown. With black markings." Her left leg shifted and pebbles rained down, pelting his head and shoulders. "It has a rattle."

He focused on her elbow, propped on the edge of the stone the upper half of her body rested upon, and racked his brain, struggling to form a mental picture, to focus. "Probably a timber rattlesnake."

"Is it venomous?"

Will dragged his teeth over his bottom lip. "Yeah." A gasp escaped her and he tacked on, "But in all the time I've lived here, I've never heard of a fatality occurring from a timber bite. Or any snakebite, for that matter."

"And how long is that?"

"That I've lived here?" At her confirmation, he continued. "All my life. Thirty-six years." He swallowed past the tight knot forming in his throat. "Chances are, he's more scared of you than you are of him. That's why he's throwing his back up. He's just telling you to keep your distance. To go your way and let him go his. Just breathe and stay calm."

She was quiet for a minute, then said, "Easy for you

to say. He's not flicking his creepy tongue three feet from your nose."

A half-hearted smile crossed his face. "Yep. I got you, and I can't say I'd rather be the one up there."

Though he'd trade places with her in a heartbeat if he had the opportunity.

Her calf muscles flexed and a heavy, somewhat exasperated breath left her. Good. Better she get mad at him than freak out and risk a snakebite. Or worse… risk knocking them both back down the rocky bank they'd spent over an hour scaling to a fate of either broken bones or death.

"Keep talking to me, Taylor," he said calmly. "Tell me what you need."

"I need to be away from this thing." Her voice cracked. "What do I do?"

The helpless plea made him long to reach up and console her. To touch her leg and reassure her that he had her back. But given the circumstances, it was best not to do anything that might startle her.

"Take a few deep breaths, look around and get your bearings," he said. "Then move slowly and carefully along the route that's the straightest line to the summit and the farthest away from him."

"Okay," she whispered.

"He's not mad at you," Will consoled. "He's just doing his morning bout of sunbathing. Go your way, and he'll go his."

"You promise?"

He tilted his head back and looked up. Mouthed silent words as a wispy cloud drifted across the blue sky above them. *Lord, please protect her. Lift her up.* "I promise."

Taylor remained frozen in place for a couple of minutes. Then her feet shifted to the right, moving slowly across the rocks she stood on, and after another minute or two, her upper body rose from its prone position on the ledge. She pulled her legs to the ledge, too, shuffled on her knees a few feet to the right, then reached up, grabbed the top ledge and hauled herself onto the summit, her long blond hair, shapely legs and colorful shoes disappearing out of sight.

"Thank You," Will whispered, glancing at the sky. Now it was time for him to ante up, too.

Steeling himself, he focused on the footholds and ledge a few feet above him and followed the same path Taylor had climbed. He reached the ledge, lifted his lower body onto it, and sure enough, there sat the timber rattlesnake, coiled like a thick inner tube, dark eyes pinned to his and rattler waving high in the air.

"What's up, buddy?" he asked softly. "You trying to give us a hard time today?"

The snake raised its head a bit higher and flicked its tongue out, the forked tip aimed directly at his forehead.

"Yeah." Will moved with slow, measured steps to the right. "You're as pretty as Taylor described."

"You two having a private moment, or you want to come up here and join me?" Taylor's blue eyes, wide and anxious between the long curtain of her hair, stared down at him from the summit and she held out her hand.

Will grinned up at her, the worried expression suffusing her pretty features as she studied him sending a wave of warmth through him. “Oh, I’m coming up.”

Sucking in a strong breath, he sprang up, grabbed the top ledge and hauled himself to the top. A soft hiss and rattle faded behind him.

Taylor grabbed his arms and pulled, and they fell back onto the flat slab of stone in a tangle of limbs. His chest hit hers and her breath left her in a whoosh as he fell on top of her.

He tucked his arms around her and, cradling the back of her helmet, rolled them over several times until they were a safe distance from the ledge. Rising up on his elbows, he looked down at her and grinned slowly. “Just for the record, you lilted twice during your episode with our little timber friend. And I guarantee your voice pitched higher than mine ever has.”

The tension in her eyes receded and she tilted her head back and laughed, the sound exhausted but infectious. “You’re probably right about that.”

Sweat sheened her brow, the cute freckles sprinkled across her nose had increased and a hefty dose of sunburn reddened her smooth cheeks.

Will lifted his free hand slowly and smoothed a wet strand of blond hair from her forehead. “You did good back there,” he said softly. “Real good. Thanks for trusting me.”

Her laughter faded and her gaze traveled over his face, a look of warmth entering her blue eyes that moved him more than he’d expected. “Thank you for keeping me going.”

Chapter Five

Normally, Taylor would've panicked by now. Pinned flat on her back to hard stone beneath a muscular, six-foot-two man had a tendency to provoke her defenses—as it had last night by the riverbank when Will had revived her. But at the moment, the firm weight of Will's thighs resting on hers and the gentle support of his warm palm cupping the back of her neck felt comforting. Almost…safe?

Will looked down at her, the amusement sparkling in his brown eyes dimming and a rueful expression crossing his face. "Sorry. Didn't mean to crush you."

He lifted his large frame off her and sat upright, tugging her with him. Seemingly assured she'd regained her balance and was comfortably seated, he released the back of her neck and backed a few feet away.

Immediately, Taylor missed the secure press of his touch and the warmth of his palm against her hair. Which was ridiculous, really. She barely knew him, had only just met him yesterday, and had no intention of lowering her guard with him now. But still…

She touched her nape and her fingers sifted through the strands of her hair, smoothing over her skin where a faint trace of his touch still lingered.

"Did I hurt you?"

Taylor glanced at him. The worried tone in his voice stirred a pleasant sense of affection within her. One she hadn't felt in years. "No."

"I was rough last night when I helped you by the bank." He frowned, his lean cheeks flushing. "I panicked, so I wasn't as gentle as I should've been when I gave you compressions. And just now, I didn't mean to drag you across the ground or make you feel—"

"You didn't hurt me," she said softly.

"Not at all?"

She smiled. "No."

His shoulders sagged and a low breath escaped his parted lips, his relief almost palpable. "That's good, then."

He removed his helmet and rubbed the dark stubble on his jaw with a shaky hand. His dark hair, sticking up in adorable tufts, ruffled in the breeze.

Taylor had the surprising urge to scoot closer to his side and smooth the wavy strands back into place. Instead, she bent her upper body over her legs, stretching her thighs, calves and arms for a few minutes, and watched as Will did the same. Her hands shook as she stretched farther and touched her toes, her thumbs and forefingers stained with dried blood.

Will stood, glanced around and pointed at a large

rock near the rapids. "There's a low boulder over there, where we can dip our feet in the river safely. Maybe wash our faces and cool off before we hike upriver. There's no way we can cross the rapids here. We'll have to hike back up into the mountains until we find a safe place to cross the river to reach the other side of the bank. It's best we rest a few minutes before we tackle that."

Nodding, Taylor removed her helmet, then joined Will by the rapids.

He placed one foot in the center of the low boulder, kept his other leg planted on the bank and held out his hand. "May I?"

"Please." She slipped her hand in his, the supportive feel of his touch moving up her arm and relaxing her muscles as she stepped onto the boulder.

Once she was safely seated, he settled beside her, leaned down and scooped up handfuls of white water, splashing it on his face, over his head and down the back of his neck. She did the same, relishing the feel of cold mountain water pouring over her hot cheeks, neck and chest.

Taylor watched the powerful surge of water rushing toward the falls, then tipped her face up, taking in the wide blue sky and high green mountain peaks. A warm summer wind whispered through the tops of cypress trees lining the riverbank and two hawks circled high above them, coasting on the swift current.

The Smokies transformed up here. From this height, the massive bone-crushing boulders downriver looked harmless. The raging white water seemed rhythmic and soothing as it swept along carved earth, and the rugged mountain walls rising high behind them seemed powerful and majestic.

She eased back on her hands and admired the view. "Jax may have been right about one thing yesterday."

Will, splashing water on his jaw and rubbing his chin, paused and raised his brows.

"When he said there's peace here," she clarified. "That you've just got to look for it... I couldn't see that yesterday, but sitting here now, by the river instead of in it, and on top of the falls instead of stranded on the bank below, it does feel like a different place."

Sighing, Will leaned back on his hands, too, and surveyed their surroundings. "Yeah. It does."

Taylor lowered her legs closer to the spray of white water, savoring the cool mist against her sore calves and ankles. "Maybe this is the kind of view Andi had last night and this morning," she added gently. "At least, I hope so."

Will's mouth tightened and the rush of water filled the brief silence between them. "It's what I prayed for," he said. "And I'm hoping He came through on that because He's answered us at least once already."

She frowned. "What do you mean?"

The corner of his mouth lifted in a half-hearted smile. "He got us up the falls, didn't He?"

Taylor glanced at the rocky wall several feet behind them and suppressed a shiver at the thought of the snake beyond their sight, basking on a ledge in the hot sun. "I have to admit, us making it up that wall on our own did seem impossible."

Will smiled wider, flashing straight white teeth. “Crazy.”

She grinned. “Stupid.”

He laughed. “You got that right.” His dark gaze held hers, then roved slowly over her face, the appreciative gleam in his eyes making her breath catch. He moved to speak, but seemed to think better of it, ducked his head and looked away.

“Go ahead.” She tilted her head as he glanced back at her, confusion in his eyes. “Just now, what were you thinking?”

He ran a hand through his dark hair and studied the impressive landscape before them. “What we just did—” he made a sweeping motion toward the falls “—being here, sitting with you like this. It takes me back. Rolls back the years and makes me feel younger.”

“Jax mentioned that you and Andi used to run rapids and rock climb all the time together. Did you do the same when you were a teen?”

A nostalgic expression crossed his face. “Yeah. These mountains have always been home for me. I was born and raised about forty miles from this spot in Stone Creek. Not a single weekend during my childhood went by without me and some friends packing a bag and hitting a trail or river. There’s not a place in the world as precious to me as this backcountry, and I miss those carefree days of exploring these mountains.” He met her eyes again, a soft smile appearing. “Makes me wonder what it would’ve been like if you and I had met back then as kids, instead of now, under different circumstances. How easily I might’ve taken to you.”

Cheeks heating, she bit back a grin and squirmed on the rock. “You barely know me.”

He nodded slowly, amusement lacing his tone. “I know enough to know I’d have been interested.”

Well. She cleared her throat awkwardly, pleasure fluttering in her belly as she admitted silently to feeling the same way about him. Only, she wasn’t quite ready to share that. “But we didn’t meet then.”

“Nope.” He looked away, a heavy sigh escaping him. “I met Heather.”

“Andi’s mother?”

“Yeah. I fell in love with her spirit, her energy. She was a bit reckless, but she loved life and the outdoors. Enjoyed everything both had to offer. In some ways, she was a lot like you.” He glanced at her beneath his thick lashes, an apologetic look in his eyes as he said, “She was strong, independent. Kept her guard up almost all the time and had a tendency to push people away—especially me.”

Taylor stared down at her shoes. Swung her legs slowly back and forth between the boulder and spray of white water.

“But she’s very different from you in the way that she regards others,” he continued. “Last night, I was wrong to blame you for everything that’s happened and you had every right to hang back on the bank and sit this climb out. You could’ve left me to find Andi on my own, but you chose to come with me instead.” His tone hardened. “Heather would never have done that. It took me a long time to realize that she has little empathy for others, and she's already abandoned Andi once. I have no doubt she'd do it again, given the chance."

Taylor looked up, her heart clenching at the thought of Andi watching her mother leave. "How old was Andi when Heather left?"

"Eight months."

Oh, no. Andi hadn't had to watch her mother walk away. She'd never actually had the chance to get to know her mother at all. Or what it was like to have one. "And you've raised Andi on your own since then?"

Will gave a jerky nod. "Though I haven't done a good job of it. Heather and I married at eighteen. We had Andi one year later. Then Heather divorced me and was gone eight months after that. I was twenty—still a kid in a lot of ways myself—and I've spent the majority of my time since then working. I started entry-level in construction, then went to school nights and weekends over the years until I worked my way up to project manager. I've worked overtime more than not and had to pinch every penny I earned to support us both. But that's no excuse. Andi deserves better than a part-time dad. She deserves a better life than the one I've given her, and she knows it. That's why she's so desperate to get out of here and away from me as soon as she graduates from high school next summer."

Taylor picked at the dirt under her nails, hesitating. This wasn't any of her business, and she wasn't exactly sure he'd welcome her two cents, but Will vastly underestimated himself as a father.

"I'm not so sure I'd bet on that being why Andi's so anxious to leave." The expression of helplessness, pain and regret on Will's face made her ache. "Sometimes, it's not a person that's causing the hurt—" she clenched her fists "—but the place. These mountains may feel like home to you, but for Andi, maybe the place you love just brings back painful memories of a mother who didn't stay and love her back. Maybe she thinks if she leaves these mountains, she'll leave that pain behind, too."

Taylor closed her eyes briefly, recalling the anguished days, weeks, months and years that followed the morning she'd shot and killed Preston. No matter how hard she'd tried, she'd never been able to shake the pain of that day…or the years of pain before it when God had abandoned her to Preston's cruel hands, refusing to answer her prayers.

"Thing is," Taylor whispered, "the kind of pain Andi carries is impossible to shake no matter how far someone runs, and when you're alone, that's when it hurts the most."

She opened her eyes and looked at Will. Her heart warmed at the concerned look in his eyes and she allowed herself to wonder, just for a moment, how different her own life might have been if she'd met Will instead of Preston all those years ago. If she'd been blessed with the caring protection and safety Will provided, rather than the violent pain and fear Preston had brought into her life.

"Just from the short time I've spent with you," she said, holding Will's gaze, "I can see you're a great dad, who's doing the best you can. Andi is lucky to have you. And she needs you—no matter how much she may be pushing you away. Don't give up on her, because when she spends enough time alone and finally realizes she needs you, it'll be harder than ever for her to find her way back to you on her own."

Despair. Will had never felt the full impact of that emotion up close, but there was no mistaking it in Taylor's eyes an hour ago. And it wasn't just her tone. It was in the dark shadows lurking deep in her eyes, the slumping curves of her usually strong-set shoulders and the dimming of her previously bright expression. Her cheery laugh had dissolved almost immediately when he'd shared his frustrations and fears regarding Andi.

Why had he done that, anyway? What had provoked him to spill his innermost worries about his relationship with his daughter to an almost-stranger?

Will frowned as he yanked his foot free of the suck of mud and hiked farther upriver, leading the way along the sunlit riverbank as Taylor followed closely by his side. He scanned the landscape for the thousandth time, searching—unsuccessfully—for any sign of Andi, and wondered absently if maybe he'd overshared with Taylor because of what they'd been through the past twenty-four hours. Or perhaps it was because he felt a connection with her. A kind of connection he had never felt before with a woman—including Heather.

That realization alone rattled him. The last thing he needed to do was take a chance on inviting another woman into his and Andi's lives, and he'd been very careful over the past sixteen years to avoid the flirtatious glances of pretty women who'd caught his eye and politely reject dinner invitations from women with whom he'd been tempted to explore a relationship. Because involving a woman in his and Andi's lives might allow her an opportunity to hurt him and, more important, Andi all over again—just like Heather had.

Only, Taylor wasn't Heather. And the more time he spent with Taylor, the more his admiration grew.

He sneaked a glance at her, his gaze lingering a bit longer on her flushed cheeks and parted lips than he'd intended.

The pink blooming in her cheeks traveled down her graceful neck and she looked up at him, those beautiful blue eyes of hers meeting his for a brief magnetic moment before she smiled softly and refocused on the trail. Her footfalls beside him were steady, but she'd said little since they'd left the summit by the waterfall.

Not that he'd spoken much, either. At first, he'd been so surprised by her compliment by the river that he'd latched on to her words and held them close—a bit too desperately, he mused wryly.

I can see you're a great dad, Will.

Man, how he'd needed to hear that, and to hear the sentiment slip from Taylor's lips so sincerely and so warmly, he'd been at a loss for a reply. It had not, however, escaped his notice that there had been an undercurrent of profound pain in her words.

Someone had hurt her—but who? And why?

His body stiffened at the thought of someone harming Taylor even as his mind balked at spending time on thinking about Taylor's past at all. Right now, Andi needed him. That was where his attention should be—

on finding Andi. He shouldn't be focused on Taylor, no matter how attracted he may be to her or how vulnerable she seemed.

But something inside him longed to dig deeper. To try, however unsuccessfully, to coax Taylor into opening up and giving him a glimpse inside her heart so that he could offer to shoulder some of the painful burden she so obviously carried.

The kind of pain Andi carries is impossible to shake no matter how far someone runs, and when you're alone, that's when it hurts the most.

When you're alone...

"Do you have family here in Tennessee?" Will grimaced as his blunt question hovered on the summer air. Not exactly the smoothest approach to opening a personal conversation.

Taylor glanced up at him in surprise, the defensive glint he'd grown accustomed to seeing flashing in her eyes.

"Sorry." Regrouping, he spread his hands and smiled sheepishly. "I don't mean to overstep into your private life, but judging from the terrain—" he gestured toward the endless stretch of violent rapids, rugged mountain ranges and muddy bank before them "—and the distance we need to cover to reach a safe place to cross the river and find Andi, we'll be hiking for at least a day or two. I thought holding conversation might help pass the time. Guess I forgot how out of practice I am."

Her brows rose. "Out of practice?"

"Yeah. You know." He shrugged, his words catching in his throat. "Spending time with a woman."

Her mouth parted and she cast a slow look over him, her gaze sweeping over his face, chest, arms and legs. “You…” Disbelief crossed her face. “You mean you don’t—?”

“Don’t date?” His face flamed. “No. Not since before I was married eighteen years ago.”

She tilted her head and stared up at him, a blank expression crossing her face. “You classify this as a date?”

Great. Just great. Now she probably thought he was an uncouth idiot, on top of being inept at conversation. How in the world had he managed to steer the conversation here?

“No.” He dragged a hand over the increasingly painful knot forming between his shoulder blades. “I meant—”

“Because if this is a date,” she said, her lips quirking, “I’d say it’s a pretty lousy one, seeing as how you haven’t even offered a girl a glass of clean water.”

He halted midstep.

Taylor stopped two steps in front of him, faced him, then winked. “Of course, I’m not what one would label a good date, either, considering I had a hand in your daughter almost drowning, insulted you after you saved my life and almost let a snake scare me into knocking us both off a hundred-foot drop.” She trailed a hand through her long hair and frowned down at the tangled strands wound between her fingers. “Not to mention, I’m not exactly at my prettiest. My hair is filthy, I’m sweating like a pig and, well, as much as I hate to admit it, I’m pretty sure I stink a little bit.”

Will grinned. “Pigs don’t sweat all that much. You don’t stink that I can tell. And from where I’m standing—” he took her in, all five foot seven of her shapely length, then admired her charming smile that he hadn’t witnessed in all its glory until this very moment “—you’re plenty pretty to me, even if you do have mud on your chin.”

Her cute smile widened. “Thank you. And I’d say the same about you.” She dipped her head, her cheeks darkening to a deeper shade of red. “I mean, you’re easy on the eyes, too.”

That shy look almost did him in. Despite the fact that he’d failed to make her comfortable enough to offer an answer to his question while simultaneously embarrassing himself, he was glad he’d stumbled into the exchange if only for the chance of glimpsing her sense of humor…and discovering she might be as drawn to him as he was to her.

“Thanks,” he said. “And though I can’t offer you a glass of clean water, I think I might be able to find a handful of wild strawberries.”

As if on cue, her stomach growled.

Chuckling, he walked over to the thick clump of lush green bushes lining the riverbank, his own gut rumbling at the thought of food. It’d been at least sixteen hours since they’d last eaten, and they’d burned off every bit of the light lunch they’d stopped the raft to eat yesterday during the early leg of their river journey.

“Think I saw a clearing through the tree line a few feet back,” he continued. “Might take me a few minutes to dig up some berries but—”

"I'd like to come with you, please."

Will paused at the edge of the bushes, waiting as she joined him, then swept a thick clump of branches aside and gestured for her to precede him through the small clearing he'd made.

She thanked him, then paused as she passed, the soft skin of her bare arm brushing his. "Will?"

He remained still. Resisted the urge to press his thumb gently to her chin and rub away the small smudge of mud that had taken up residence there. "Yeah?"

"In answer to your question, I don't have any family," she said quietly. "Not in Tennessee or anywhere else. I married years ago and I..." Her voice faded so much her words were barely discernible. "I've been widowed for five years now."

Breath catching at her loss, he did reach out then, hesitating as her eyes met his. When she lifted her chin in silent invitation, he touched his thumb to the slight indentation and rubbed the mud away, revealing clean, soft skin.

"I'm sorry, Taylor," he whispered.

Her vulnerable gaze lowered to his mouth and lingered there a few moments before she ducked her head, dislodging his touch, and ducked past him into a small clearing peppered with thick swaths of trees and bushes.

Will followed, stopping as a breeze danced over his sweaty forehead, and admired the play of sunlight over Taylor's blond hair as she bent and poked around a low-lying set of bushes.

"There's plenty of sunlight in this meadow," he

said, glancing around the lush green clearing. "There's bound to be some wild strawberries."

"And blackberries." She straightened and held out her hand. Several plump berries filled her small palm. "How 'bout we split the first course?"

He smiled. "Sounds good."

She tipped her hand and spilled half of the blackberries into his palm. He popped a few in his mouth and closed his eyes, savoring the plump flesh and tangy juice on his parched tongue.

Taylor released a small moan of pleasure. "These are delicious."

"I second that." Will's stomach rumbled loud enough to elicit a laugh from Taylor. "Might need to find a few more, though."

Over the next half hour, they scoured a dozen more promising plants and bushes and were rewarded with several more handfuls of blackberries, wild strawberries and a few blueberries, which served as a makeshift breakfast.

"Not exactly bacon and eggs," Will said, rubbing his belly, "but that should get us by for a little while at least."

Taylor nodded and licked her lips, which were stained an adorable shade of red. "Most definitely." She smiled. "Must've been because I was starving, but those berries were the best meal I've had in a long time."

Will cocked an eyebrow. "Better than a rib-eye steak in a five-star restaurant on a first date?"

She grinned. "Mayb—"

A loud crash broke the peaceful stillness of the sunny meadow, birds scattered and two bulky figures barreled through a set of tall bushes fifty yards behind Taylor.

Will froze. “Taylor,” he whispered quietly, holding out a shaky hand. “Turn around and walk back toward me very slowly.”

Chapter Six

Eyes wide, Taylor turned slowly. There, on the opposite side of the meadow, stood two black bears, head-to-head, eyes locked. The largest bear emitted a series of aggressive grunts, ducked low, then sprang up, swiping his massive paw across the smaller bear's nose.

Immediately, the smaller bear lunged, charged head-first and wrestled with its dominant counterpart. The two rose on their hind legs, locking teeth and claws as they flung each other to and fro. Their black hides rippled in the sunlight, thick clumps of fur flew in all directions and fragile branches broke under the animals' muscular bulk.

Taylor backed toward Will, her arms stiff by her sides. Her feet moved blindly behind her, stumbling over slippery mud and tangled twigs, and she reached back with one arm, her fingers searching for Will's hand.

His warm palm closed around hers and tugged, guiding her back a few feet until she reached his side.

Edging in front of her, Will pressed one long leg against hers and nudged her into slow, measured steps in the direction of the riverbank.

The battle between the bears continued. Growls, cracks and crashes echoed around the tree-lined clearing.

Taylor glanced over her shoulder. The mud-slicked bank they'd traveled lay a mere five feet behind them now, each careful step they took bringing them closer to a safer distance from the angry bears.

She gripped Will's solid biceps with her free hand, drawing comfort from his solid strength, then whispered, "We're almost there. Five more feet to the tree line and one more foot after that to the bank."

His hand tightened around hers in response.

The chaos ceased. Having managed to writhe its way free from the clutch of the dominant bear, the smaller bear dived through crushed bushes and hustled out of sight.

Four feet. Taylor glanced behind her once more and bit her lip. Three, now.

Sharp popping sounds rang out across the clearing, echoing against the tree line. Ears back, the dominant bear, facing them, stood motionless and eyed them from afar. The popping noise continued as the bear clacked his molars together and pawed the ground.

Black eyes, angry and intent, pinned to Taylor's face, surveying, measuring…weighing whether or not to attack. His lips drew back, daggerlike teeth emerged and a deep growl rumbled in the animal's wide chest.

Strangely, Preston's angry hiss whispered through

her mind, rolling through her on a familiar wave of debilitating fear.

Don't move. Stay right there, and I'll come to you.

Her legs froze, still three feet from the tree line and four from the riverbank. A sensation of terror snaked up her spine and wound about her like a massive fist, tightening around her throat, constricting her lungs and spurring goose bumps on her flesh. She could easily recall the feel of the hard kitchen tile beneath her back as he'd approached. Feel the desperate urge to flee at the same time her limbs refused to move.

"Taylor?"

When you make mistakes, Taylor, you have to pay for them. It's the only way to learn.

"Taylor." Will squeezed her hand hard and, gaze trained on the bear, spoke in low tones. "Keep walking to the side and back slowly. He's wound up and on the defensive. We're just in the wrong place at the wrong time." Will straightened and rolled his shoulders, the protective posture of his muscular back lifting, edging fully in front of her and obscuring her vision. "We're leaving now, buddy. We'll be out of your hair in just a sec."

Body trembling, she tried to focus on the baritone of Will's calm voice and forced her feet to move again. They resumed backing away, covering three more feet of muddy ground until they finally reached the tree line.

A branch poked sharply into Taylor's back and she rose to her toes and peered over Will's shoulder. The bear stood where it had moments before, hunched low to the ground, staring them down.

Slowly, Taylor reached back with her free hand, lifted the branch overhead and slipped underneath. Mud squelched beneath her shoes and her legs faltered, sliding unsteadily.

"Will," she urged softly, lifting the branch higher and tugging his elbow. "Come on."

He eased beneath the branch and joined her on the bank, then cupped her raised forearm with his palm and helped her lower the branch. Thick stems and wide leaves slowly curtained the bear's glare.

The urge to run shot through Taylor's veins, but she linked hands with Will instead and continued taking slow, measured steps sideways up the riverbank. Beyond the tree line, twigs snapped, leaves rustled and sporadic glimpses of the bear's dark fur appeared between gaps in the tree line.

"He's following us." Taylor's throat felt raw, her words leaving her in shaky bursts.

Will kept his gaze on the bear's movements behind the thick foliage and raised his voice over the roar of the rapids beside them. "What's behind us? Is the path clear?"

She gripped his hand with both of hers and looked over her shoulder. "No. There's a sharp incline filled with rocks and it merges with trees. There are low branches, thick brush."

Rustling continued behind the trees, drawing closer.

Will raised their entwined hands above their heads and spoke louder. "If he charges, don't run—that'll provoke him. Stand your ground, shout him down and fight. Throw your back up and try to look bigger than he is. It's the only way to scare him off."

The rhythmic crash of branches and leaves beyond the tree line slowed with each of Will's words. An eerie stillness settled over the bear's hulking form as he stopped moving and watched them retreat.

"There's something wrong with him," Taylor said, waving her arms alongside Will as they increased the distance between them and the bear. "He should've run from us by now, but he's not afraid of us. He's—"

"Predatory." Will's mouth tightened, his eyes sharpening on the tree line. "And the two of us would fill his gut a whole lot more than those berries he trampled." Releasing her hand, he reached back and pressed his palm to her middle, nudging her farther back. "Find a path through the brush behind us and get a head start, but don't turn your back."

"No. I won't leave you."

"You're not leaving me." He glanced over his shoulder, his warm gaze meeting hers. "You're helping me. Helping us." His big palm pushed her again as he turned his head and refocused on the dark hulking figure poised several feet away. "Go, Taylor. Keep your eyes this way and make a path for us."

She hesitated, her attention torn between Will's strong hand pressing against her belly and the imposing figure lurking among the trees.

"Please go," Will repeated, raising his arms back over his head in a warding-off motion.

Branches rustled along the tree line, and Taylor, galvanized by a surge of adrenaline, took one unsteady step backward, then another…and another, until her outstretched arm met the soft brush of leaves.

Feet stumbling over an uneven pile of rocks, she felt her way back through the thick underbrush. Thorns scraped her bare thighs and low-hanging branches ensnared her hair, yanking hard, delivering sharp stings to her scalp as she passed, but she forged on, breaking thin branches, stomping tangled shrubs and carving a path for Will, who fell farther and farther behind.

She reached the end of the thicket of trees, bushes and rocks, and the familiar suck of mud returned as her thin water shoes settled into the wet riverbank. Grabbing a thick, low-hanging branch closest to her, she wedged her shoulder underneath it, forced it up, then waited, watching as Will crouched and traced her steps, easing his way back through gnarled branches and sharp stones.

"This way," she beckoned, her pulse pounding in her ears, melding with the roar of white water that surged along the rapids beside her. "There's an opening right behind you. About seven feet back."

Will, still crouching low, worked his way through the tangled brush, ducked beneath the branch she'd raised and stilled by her side.

They waited. Listened. Water splashed over boulders and crashed along the riverbank. Birds chirped overhead, and a squirrel wound its way up the thick trunk of a nearby birch tree. But the rhythmic rustle of the bear's movements had stopped and the sinister feel of its stalking presence receded.

"I think it's gone," Will said quietly. He eased back on his haunches and exhaled. Blood trickled over his left biceps and streamed in thin rivulets down his tanned forearm.

"You're hurt." Taylor lifted his arm and inspected the blood trail, seeking the source.

Will joined her, probing along the injury on his upper arm with his fingertips. "It's nothing—just a cut. A thorn caught me on the way through."

"It *is* something," she said. "Something bad enough to bleed at least." She grabbed the hem of her T-shirt, located the cleanest section of cloth and tore the fabric, ripping a long strip free. "Lift your arm out, please."

He did as she requested, his soft breaths whispering through her hair as she bent over his injury, wrapped the cloth around his biceps and tied a knot, securing it into a makeshift bandage.

"There," she said softly. "That'll at least help stop the bleeding."

His fingers brushed her temple, stroked her damp hair back over her shoulder. Then his warm palm cupped her cheek. "Are you all right?"

The gentle caress of his touch and low throb of his voice almost coaxed her into sagging against him, resting her head on his wide chest and sinking into his protective embrace.

Almost…

"I'm okay." Her voice, when it finally emerged from her constricted throat, sounded gravelly. She cleared her throat, gently removed his hand from her cheek and stood. “We better get going. Put some more distance between us and the bear.”

She didn’t wait for him to follow, but headed off instead, taking brisk—if slightly unsteady—steps across the muddy bank and up the increasing incline of the winding bank. So much for wanting to keep her distance from him. Every moment she spent with him in this wild backcountry revealed another layer of his caring nature, protective instincts and gruff tenderness she’d never found in a man before. Any one of those attributes would be enough to attract a woman’s attention, much less all three at once.

After a few moments, his heavy tread fell in step beside her and she could feel his gaze on her. His careful inspection of her expression made her cheeks burn and her skin tingle where the gentle support of his palm still lingered.

They continued walking in silence, slipping over wet stretches of the bank where puddles of rain had accumulated overnight and climbing over tall piles of stones and boulders along bends in the river. Last night’s storm had dumped so much rain into the river the white water swelled twice as high as it had the night before, each set of rapids barreling faster down the landscape and leaving no safe place to cross the river.

Three hours later, they’d covered almost two and a half miles, stopping every half mile to scan their surroundings and call out to Andi. They received no response, and each time silence greeted Will’s calls for his daughter, his expression darkened, his hopes visibly dimming. Which was no wonder, considering what they'd just been up against. If they'd run into an aggressive black bear here, there was every chance Andi may have run into one wherever she was now.

Taylor stumbled midstep. That terrifying thought alone would be too much for any loving father to endure.

Soon, the sun rose high in the sky and heat beat down on their heads and shoulders. Taylor paused, wiped her sweaty forehead with the back of her hand and plucked her damp T-shirt from her midriff, fanning it away from her skin and creating a breeze against her sweat-slicked abs.

"We've covered a lot of ground." Will stopped beside her and dragged his hand through his wet hair. "Almost three miles, if I've calculated correctly. We can rest here for a while, if you'd like, then head farther upriver. See if there might be a safer place to cross?"

Taylor shook her head. "I'm good if you want to conti—"

Will lifted a hand, halting her speech, then looked away and tilted his head. "Do you hear that?"

In the distance, a soft beating sound emerged. The rhythmic whooshing grew more distinct as it drew closer, transforming into a strong pulse of power that rebounded crisply off nearby mountain peaks.

Taylor's pulse kicked up a notch and her eyes widened as she met Will's gaze, an equally excited hope returning to his expression.

He smiled. "Rescue chopper."

Will could barely suppress the renewed energy charging through his veins at the thought of a helicopter approaching. Automatically, his feet slipped and slid over the muddy riverbank as he lunged forward, running toward the sound of whirling blades.

"It's up ahead," he shouted over his shoulder. "Just around the bend, from the sounds of it."

Maybe Jax, Beth and Martin had fared better than he'd assumed. Maybe they'd made it out of the rapids and hiked far enough upriver to reach a cell signal, call for help and summon a rescue chopper in their direction. Maybe—his heart slammed against his ribs—Andi had already been rescued. Maybe it wasn't such a stretch of hope to imagine she sat in the chopper now, miles above him, looking safely down on the wilds of the Smokies.

Please let her be there, he prayed silently.

Taylor's voice, a mere wisp of a sound that faded even more with each of his pounding steps, barely broke through the wind whistling past his ears. "Wait!"

He kept running. Jumped over a scattering of sharp rocks lining the bank. Ducked beneath the low sprawling limb of a spruce tree. Something sharp jabbed his cheek. He swiped at it and pressed on.

The tree line fell back and a mud-slicked bank appeared again. He stomped through it, tilting his head back as he ran, and scanned the sky. There, about two hundred yards out, he spotted the barest outline of an approaching helicopter high above.

"There it is!" he shouted.

He glanced around wildly, registering a steep, densely foliaged embankment on the opposite side of the river and a less imposing bluff to his right. No way would the pilot catch a glimpse of him here, wedged between two high banks, hidden beneath dense vegetation and overshadowed by the roaring force of the river.

The bluff's sloping face—though mud-slicked—was scarcely populated with trees and bushes…but scalable. And the only other option was to stand here beside the rapids, stare helplessly at an unreachable sky and hope that the pilot passing above would glance his way.

Nope. This might be the best chance he had of reaching Andi today. He had no choice but to try.

Sprinting toward the base of the bluff, he waved an arm in Taylor's direction. "Stay here. I'm gonna try to get as close as I can."

"Please, Will. Don't g…"

Taylor's words faded away as he dug his hands into the muddy bluff, grabbed a handful of wet earth and hauled his body onto the sloping face. Keeping close to the ground, he yanked his hands and feet from the mud and climbed higher. Faster. Seeking out drier sections of earth as he ascended, straining to maintain his grip, reaching with his right arm, then left. Climbing higher and higher.

The whir of helicopter blades drew closer. Body jerking on a bolt of urgency, he sprang up, swiped at the trunk of a river birch—and missed!

Wet ground gave way beneath his feet and he slid haphazardly downward, gaining speed, his arms scrambling for a secure hold. Then, abruptly, he stopped.

He glanced down, his eyes meeting Taylor's.

She blinked up at him, pain flooding her pretty features as she stiffened her upper body and repositioned her foot against the trunk of a birch below her. Her left shoulder and back wedged tighter against his right hip and thigh, providing a stable support for the right half of his body.

He stared down at her, momentarily taken aback by her strength, relief and admiration surging through him.

"You wanna get your bearings back?" Her voice trembled and she grimaced under the increasing pressure of his weight as he slid farther down. "I can't brace you here forever."

Immediately, he renewed his hold on a somewhat dry section of ground and yanked, lifting part of his weight off Taylor and heaving himself upward.

The helicopter approached, its underside barely visible through a clump of branches above him in the distance.

Will stretched his arm out, reaching for a higher handhold, when a sharp crack rang out high above and an increasingly loud crash barreled down the sloping bluff.

"Oh, no," he whispered hoarsely, craning his head around to look down at Taylor. "Go back, Taylor!"

"What?" Frowning, she stopped midclimb, then froze as her gaze swept past him toward the top of the bluff.

"Go back," he shouted. "Mudslide!"

The word had barely escaped his lips when the earth shifted beneath his hands and a heavy tangle of slimy mud, uprooted trees and crushed deadfall waved down the slope, slamming into them.

Will shifted his weight, throwing himself onto his back, and did his best to control his descent toward Taylor, his body shifting and sliding rapidly along mud and loose soil. Debris swept past him and plunged over Taylor, sweeping her away from her safe perch against a tree trunk and tumbling her down the bluff.

Shoving off with his hands, Will maneuvered himself in Taylor's direction, reached her side and shot his hand out, grabbing her arm and hauling her to his side. He wrapped one arm around her waist, tucked her cheek to his chest and covered the back of her head with his hand, protecting her as best as he could against the onslaught of debris rolling over and under them.

A sharp cry escaped her, and she curled her fists into his T-shirt and wrapped one of her legs around one of his, holding on as they sped down the sloping embankment.

Wood cracked, leafy branches swept past them and stones of various sizes bounced in every direction, narrowly missing his head.

"Will!"

Frantic, Taylor clutched him closer as they tumbled, twisted and rolled at full speed. The roar of the rapids rushed closer and the hard mud-slicked bank and boulders flashed below.

Will's throat closed. This was it. They'd come as far as they'd ever get. At the speed they traveled and height they plummeted, their bodies would slam against the rocks, shattering their bones and cracking their skulls. And if they were lucky enough to be carried over the boulders by plunging earth, they'd be thrown into the river and tossed along the rapids, most likely drowning minutes after they hit the white water.

A panicked, humorless laugh burst from his lips. In moments, they'd be right back where they started, at the mercy of the water, gasping for breath as violent white water snatched their life by slow, cold degrees of suffocation.

Andi. Will tried to open his eyes, tried to focus on the blue sky swirling above, his view impeded by each rolling wave of thick mud and painful dig of tumbling debris. The whir of helicopter blades disappeared and the roar of sliding earth filled his ears, drowning out every ounce of hope that still whispered in his soul.

Andi. He'd failed her, and may never see her again.

Chapter Seven

Taylor flinched as a broken branch dug into her waist, tightened her fists on Will's shirt and pressed her cheek against the base of his throat.

"Andi…" His warm skin vibrated against her cheek on the hoarse whisper, his words laced with pain and desperation.

Mud shoved them farther down the embankment and coated their arms and legs. She squeezed her eyes shut and savored the protective strength of Will's arms around her and hand cradling the back of her head. Gratitude swept through her on an oddly comforting sensation.

Wherever they landed, whatever happened next… at least, this time, she wasn't alone.

The heavy crash of debris raining down around them was overcome with the roar of water.

The river. Taylor tensed. They were headed straight for the river.

Their descent continued, the muddy earth beneath

their bodies slipping, sliding, then flinging them through the air. Memories of rocks and hard ground flashed through her mind, sending a fresh wave of panic through her. Her stomach dropped and her muscles tensed in preparation for impact.

Icy water smacked against her limbs and face, surged over her head and sucked her body farther downward until her feet hit hard earth—the riverbed, maybe?—and her legs buckled beneath her.

Weightless, her limbs jerked up, pulled along a swift current that lifted her body and rolled her to a supine position. Her face broke the water's surface and she dragged in a lungful of air, her throat burning. She reached out, grasping for a renewed hold on Will, but her hands only met water and rocks.

"W-Will!" Her lips, cold and wet, trembled. She licked away a fresh spray of white water and tried to regain her bearings.

Wispy clouds and blue sky flew past overhead. Green foliage, blurry, sped by in her peripheral vision. She kicked her legs and stroked her arms, just managing to lift her head and scan her surroundings.

Boulders, steep drops and the spray of white water filled her vision. Bracing, she lowered her head as the rapids plunged her over a series of drops that seemed to go on and on.

She cleared a drop and the rapids spit her out to a smoother stretch of water. Raising her head again, she immediately recognized the angry churn of the falls.

"No!" Taylor beat fiercely against the water with her legs and arms, straining to regain control.

They'd made it safely over the falls once; there were no guarantees they'd escape unscathed a second time. And Will…

Panic surged in her chest as she frantically looked around. Where was he?

Up ahead, to the right, a thick log protruded from the bank. Taylor kicked and swam against the fierce current, stretched out her arms and lunged, managing to grab the log. She dug her nails in and pulled her upper body onto it.

"Will," she shouted, scanning the area for any sign of him.

Water swept past, dipping over low falls and churning around boulders. A minute passed, then another and another, each second stretching into an eternity.

Where was he? Surely he'd traveled the same path she had. They'd been holding on to each other when they'd hit the water.

Her mouth ran dry as another thought occurred to her. What if he'd traveled ahead of her? What if he'd already plunged over the falls?

Mouth parting, she stared downriver at the point where white water converged, sped up and dropped over a steep edge, out of sight. If he'd plunged over the falls alone, he could be at the bottom of the gorge now—unconscious like she had been last night. At the mercy of the water. Stranded alone like his daughter.

Andi…

Taylor froze, the painful tone of Will's voice as he'd called for his daughter minutes earlier still fresh on her mind…and heart.

No. She shook her head, a sob rising in her throat, and lowered her chin to the log. Will loved Andi so much—Taylor had recognized that almost immediately after meeting the two of them. For Will and Andi to lose each other like this—

"Please, God…" Her voice surprised her, the hesitant words she whispered out loud, amid the vicious roar of white water, pouring from a deep-seated ache in her chest. "Please bring Will to safety. Please let him and Andi survive this and find each other."

She hadn't spoken to God directly in so long she wasn't sure if He heard her. And she had no idea if He would even answer someone like her. Why should He when she'd lived apart from Him for so long?

I've lived without Him...and I've lived with Him.

Taylor closed her eyes and breathed deep, drawing strength from the memory of Will's words.

I keep talking to Him and He comes through one way or another.

"Please," she pleaded again. "Will's a good, faithful man. He deserves all the help You're willing to give. Please help him. For his sake, if not for mine."

"Taylor!"

Her eyes sprang open. She bolted upright and swiveled her head in the direction of the shout. It originated upriver. Somewhere to the lef—

"Will," she shouted back, a wide smile fighting its way to her lips.

There he was, floating on his back, feetfirst, around a sharp bend, being swept swiftly along the current in her direction.

Taylor stretched over the log and reached out with one hand, her other arm wrapped snugly around the log beneath her. “Swim over as close as you can! I’ll grab you and pull you in!”

Will rolled over and swam vigorously in Taylor’s direction, his dark eyes darting between her and the rapidly approaching falls, then back again. A panicked urgency suffused his expression as his progress slowed, the powerful rapids yanking him in another direction.

He glanced at the falls again, his eyes moving over various paths along the water, a worried look appearing. The current moved fast, dragging him closer and closer to the impending drop.

“You trust me?” she shouted.

His dark gaze met hers and his mouth parted soundlessly.

“I won’t leave you!” She stretched her arm out farther, her fingers grasping in his direction. “If you go over, I’ll follow. We’re in this together, I promise.” A fierce energy swept over her and entered her voice. “Do you trust me?”

He drew closer, the window of opportunity narrowing. A look of resolution entered his eyes. “Yes.”

“Then do it!”

He lunged out of the water toward her, but the rapids yanked him back, causing him to fall short half a foot.

She managed to snag his upper arm as he passed, her fingers curling tightly around his biceps. He latched on to her arm in return, his hand grasping her upper arm, as well.

His weight pulled her upper body down to the edge

of the log. She wrapped her legs around it and hooked her feet at the ankles, straining to maintain her grip as he pulled toward her.

When he drew close, he grabbed the log with his free hand, yanked himself out of the swift-moving current and hauled his body along it and onto shore.

Taylor released his arm once he had his bearings, shoved herself upright and carefully crawled backward along the log.

"Taylor." A strong arm wrapped around her waist and lifted her from the log. "Hold on to me."

Moments later, she was pressed tight to Will's side and she curled her arms around his shoulders as he dragged them onto the riverbank. They lay still for a couple of minutes, their chests heaving with labored breaths, and raspy coughs escaped them sporadically.

Soon, Taylor's breathing calmed and the burning sensation in her lungs subsided. She stared up at the blue sky, the bright late-afternoon sun warm on her skin and a small, unfamiliar feeling unfurling within her.

"He answered me," she whispered.

It was silent for a moment, save for the rush of the river.

Will shifted beside her, his legs moving restlessly. She rolled her head to the side and met his eyes.

His brow furrowed. "What'd you say?"

"I said, He answered me." Smiling, she added softly, "When I made it out of the water, I couldn't see you. I didn't know where you were. If you'd gone over the falls or—" Her voice broke and a relieved laugh burst from her lips. "I was so scared and I had no idea what to do. So I did what you said. I kept talking to Him. I prayed and asked Him to help you. To help Andi." Her smile widened. "And there you were. You just came out of nowhere, calling my name."

She tipped her head back and looked up at the sky again, a silent prayer of gratitude moving through her mind. "I've never heard Him answer me before. But He answered this time."

Another breeze swept over the river, bending the trees that lined the bank and cooling her wet skin. The gentle feel of it strengthened that pleasant sensation blooming in her chest.

A growl of frustration erupted beside her and Will shot to his feet.

Startled by his abrupt movement, Taylor sat up as he paced quickly in front of her, stalking in one direction, then the other, narrowing his eyes at the mountain range in the distance.

"You call this an answer?" His hands balled into fists by his sides and an angry hiss escaped him. "This isn't an answer," he said through gritted teeth. "Don't you see where we are?" He waved an arm in the air, stabbing his hand at the falls. "We're right back where we started. We scaled a wall and spent the better part of the day hiking almost four miles just to end up right back where we were hours ago."

Taylor's smile slowly faded.

His expression contorted in anger and his voice hardened. "There's no way that pilot saw us—if it even was a rescue chopper. Andi's already spent one night alone in the middle of nowhere, injured. There's no way we can regain the ground we've lost just now. We've got no shelter, no supplies, no food or clean water. And you call this an answer?"

Heart breaking at the fear in his tone, she looked down and twisted the hem of her T-shirt. Water spilled from it and splashed against a rock beside her. "I only meant—"

"What?" Will bit out. "What did you mean? That He did us a favor? Andi is miles away, alone in back-country. That bear you and I saw earlier today—" he swept his arm toward the sprawling landscape at his back "—that's only a peek of what's out there. The best estimate I've ever heard for this area suggests there's two bears roaming every couple of square miles surrounding us. There are at least three miles standing between me and my daughter right now."

Pain laced his tone and his chin trembled. He spun away and tilted his head back, the knuckles of his clenched fists turning white by his sides.

"You call this an answer?" he shouted to the sky. "How could You do it? Andi needed You and—" Voice cracking, he raked a hand through his thick hair, then bent, grabbed a loose stone from the bank and hurled it into the rapids.

Taylor watched as the stone smacked into a spray of white water, skipped over the swell of a wave, then bounced onto the opposite bank. It settled on a smooth stretch of rock—close to where she and Will had sat hours earlier, relishing their success of scaling the wall and evading a snake.

She stood, her smile slowly returning. "You done with that temper tantrum of yours? Because if you are, there's something you should know."

Will stiffened, the angry panic shooting through him intensifying at the sound of Taylor's chipper tone. When he faced her, the bright smile spreading across her face only made it worse.

"You good now?" she asked, grinning wider. "Because I want to make sure you hear what I'm about to tell you."

What could she possibly say right now to make this right? And what in the world did she have to smile about? Here they were, stranded in the middle of nowhere with next to no chance of reaching Andi before tomorrow, and she somehow managed to find humor in the situation?

He swallowed an angry retort—along with a good, healthy dose of pride—and nodded slowly. "Go ahead."

"We're not in exactly the same place we were hours ago," she explained calmly, motioning toward the river behind his back. "We're on the opposite side of the river than we were this morning. We're on the same side Andi is on now."

He glanced over his shoulder and stared across the rapids at the smooth stone he'd sat on with Taylor hours before, divulging his secrets and fears, drawing comfort from her consoling words. Then he spun around and studied the unfamiliar stretch of riverbank and thick forest that lay before them now—a completely different view than the one he and Taylor had faced this morning.

"We don't have to find a place to cross the river now," Taylor continued. "That mudslide..." She grimaced. "It wasn't my favorite part of the day so far, but it did the trick. It threw us to the other side of the river."

Will looked at the new terrain before them for a few more moments, then studied her face, a hesitant note entering his voice. "That's only a good thing if Andi made it across the rocks to the bank."

Her expression gentled, an understanding light entering her eyes. "Is Andi as stubborn as you?"

His lips twitched despite the residual fear and anger simmering inside him. "Yeah. She's twice as stubborn."

"Then she definitely made it. And I'd say that's a pretty good answer for the situation we're in right now."

Yep. She had a point. God had given them an answer—he'd just been too angry and stubborn to see it. Instead, he'd railed against God and Taylor, blaming them both for Andi's predicament. That alone was enough to shame him.

Face burning, he ducked his head and kneaded the back of his neck. "I..." He cleared his throat and tried again. "I'm sorry. I don't usually lose my cool like that. I never intended to offend you. Or scare you. Or—"

"It's okay," she said softly. "You don't have to apologize. You're a great dad and you're worried for your daughter. I understood." She tilted her head, her gaze drifting over him slowly, and a look of surprise moved through her expression. "And you didn't scare me."

Her blue eyes met his and a blush bloomed along her freckled cheeks. “I’m not afraid when I’m with you.”

The weight of her admission hung on the air between them. Something in her tone—awe or wonder, maybe?—unsettled him. He watched her face, an ache spreading through him at the wounded vulnerability in her eyes.

“Taylor. Has someone h—?”

“We better get moving.” She looked away, that brief flash of vulnerability masked and set aside, almost as though it had never existed. “The sun’ll set in a couple of hours, and we need to find a place to bed down for the night, don’t you think?”

He moved to answer, but she turned away, stepped carefully over the rocks scattered along the riverbank and began hiking into the woods ahead.

Will rolled his shoulders and stretched the strained muscles in his arms and legs, then followed in her wake, contemplating all the while what—*or who*—had put that look in Taylor’s eyes.

For over an hour, they hiked through thick forest, ducking beneath leafy branches, forcing their way through thorny underbrush and climbing over fallen trees. A sore, tender feeling began to spread through Will’s arms and legs, weighing him down and slowing his steps. He couldn’t help but notice that Taylor’s previously energetic pace had waned, as well.

Will, breathing deeply, stopped as they reached a small clearing and took stock of their surroundings. “This might be a good place to set up camp for the night.” He motioned at the woods surrounding them across the meadow. "There's plenty of deadfall and a sturdy oak over there where we can set up a lean-to for the night."

Taylor wiped her brow and sighed. "Sounds good to me. What would you like me to do?"

Her shoulders sagged and the color in her face had receded, her complexion having paled slightly. There was an almost imperceptible tremor running through her legs—not much, but enough that he noticed.

Will frowned. All of that was to be expected. She'd climbed two embankments, tumbled down a mudslide, dragged herself and him out of the river and had hiked at least five miles today with little food and no clean water. And yesterday's drama was in addition to today's challenges. It was a miracle they'd made it as far as they had.

He winced. "Look, you've got to be exhausted. Why don't you sit and rest while I take care of the lean-to?"

She closed her eyes and leaned her head back, her face tilted to catch the fading glow of the sun, which slowly lowered below the horizon in the distance. "Aren't you tired, too?"

The graceful curve of her neck caught his eye, and he watched as a bead of sweat trickled down from her nape, veered over her shoulder and settled in the gentle dip within her collarbone. An errant strand of her hair fluttered in the breeze and caught on her thick eyelashes. He admired her elegant profile for a moment, then tore his gaze away and looked down instead, kicking a large pine cone that rested beside his shoe.

"Yeah." His voice sounded husky. He cleared his throat, rubbed his palms over his thighs and smiled.

"To be honest with you, if I stretched out on the ground right now, I wouldn't be able to move again for at least ten hours."

"Then we'll both build the lean-to." A twig snapped as she faced him, her clear blue eyes brightened by her grin, and her pretty features drew him in again. "Together," she added softly.

Together. His smile grew so much his sunburned cheeks smarted. He liked the sound of that word on Taylor's lips. A whole lot more than he'd expected.

"I'll take you up on that." His conscience told him to stop there, to resist voicing any more thoughts aloud and avoid hinting at any ounce of sentimentality. But the emotions welling within him tumbled off his own lips before he could halt them. "I won't say I'm glad we're stuck out here, but if I had to be in this position again, I can't say I'd want anyone else by my side other than you. You're an amazing woman, Taylor Holt. I hope you know that."

The bright spark in her blue eyes started to fade and her grin slipped.

What was wrong in what he'd said? Had he offended her? He hoped not. Despite not knowing which words had hurt her, his hands rose slightly as if to take them back. To gather them up and hide them away. If for no other reason than to see that relaxed look of happiness return to her expression.

"I used to think so," she whispered. "A long time ago."

She walked away, her long blond hair swinging gently across her back. She bent and picked up a sturdy dead branch off the forest bed. "Is this a good length for the support beam of the lean-to you're planning?"

He shrugged. "It'll do fine. Tayl—?"

"Can we just focus on the lean-to for now?" Her voice trembled and she dipped her head, avoiding his eyes. "Please?"

Will hesitated, wanting to continue the conversation. Wanting to ask more questions—any she'd allow him to—just so long as she opened up to him a bit more. But clearly, she wasn't ready for that.

"Of course," he said softly. "Whatever you want."

Collecting branches, snapping each to the right length and arranging them into the formation of a slanted roof between the trunks of two oak trees took over an hour and sapped the last bit of strength left in Will's body.

"Well," he said, inspecting the crude shelter, "it's definitely not a five-star hotel, but it'll get us through the night." Spotting a large gap in between two logs, he sighed and looked up. Dusk had fallen and there were no clouds in the slowly darkening sky, which eased his worries a bit. "There'll be a big gap over our heads, but there aren't any clouds, so no chance of rain tonight, that I can tell. We could pile some moss over the top if you'd like? Just to be safe?"

Taylor shook her head and smiled. "Nah. It's summer, so it won't get too chilly tonight, and besides, I kinda like the gap. It's like a moon roof. Or a little window to the stars."

Will laughed. "That's a nice way of looking at it." He waved a hand at the wide opening. "After you."

She slipped under the small roof and settled on the ground, a heavy sigh of exhaustion escaping her. Will followed suit and sat beside her.

"The house itself might not be worth market price," Taylor said, her gaze moving slowly over the scenery before them, "but the view is worth a mil."

He followed her gaze, his body relaxing as he took in the sights before them. The sun had dipped below the horizon and a glorious blaze of color spread across the night sky, then slowly receded, casting a pink and lavender glow over the misty meadow in front of them.

Trees rustled on the other side of the clearing. Will sat up straighter, his hands clenching against his thighs as the low rumble of the bear from hours earlier returned to his mind. But then two figures emerged, one large and one small, gracefully making their way into the center of the meadow, and emotion washed over him.

"Taylor," he whispered, touching her forearm. "Look."

There, just visible amid the light mist settling over the clearing, a mother elk and calf strolled across the damp ground, bent their heads and grazed soundlessly several feet away.

"Oh, how beautiful," Taylor whispered. Blue eyes on the elk, her hand sought his, her warm fingers slipping between his and her soft palm pressing snugly to his own. She watched quietly for a few minutes, then said softly, "Maybe it's another answer. One we haven't been looking for." Her tone was thin. Uncertain, but laced with a thread of hope he hadn't heard in her voice before. "Maybe this is His way of telling us there are more good things to come."

Under the increasing fall of darkness, she leaned more heavily against him. He lifted his arm carefully, slid it around her shoulders, and she drifted into sleep, her cheek resting against his chest. Her slow, steady pulse, beating rhythmically just beneath her skin, mingled with his own, their heartbeats a soothing sensation between their joined palms.

There were no more questions and no more answers. No more conversation of any kind for the rest of the night. But as sleep tugged heavily at Will, he couldn't help but smile, despite the fears he still harbored for Andi's safety. Just the feel of Taylor's even breaths whispering over his chest, the warm weight of her pressing against his side and the hint of hope in her words—the thought that God would help them make it out of this…and find Andi—was enough to calm his worries for the night.

Chapter Eight

Warmth bloomed over Taylor's skin and a soft orange glow seeped through her closed eyelids. She stirred slowly, breathing deeply, and opened her eyes.

A white T-shirt lay beneath her cheek and the muscular curve of Will's chest supported her head, lifting slightly with each of his slow breaths. Carefully, so as not to disturb him, she removed her palm from his shoulder and sat up.

His even breathing paused. Then his chest rose on a deep inhalation and he rolled his head to the side, settling when he found a more comfortable position against the logs forming the wall of the lean-to at his back.

Taylor smiled and watched him silently for a few moments, admiring the relaxed sprawl of his toned limbs and peaceful set of his handsome features.

She studied his tousled hair, defined cheekbones, stubbled jaw and wide chest. Last night, she'd been so exhausted that she'd fallen asleep moments after sitting beneath the lean-to. Her last memory before drifting off had been enjoying the sight of elk grazing in the meadow as the sun had slowly disappeared behind the mountain range in the distance. Soon after, she'd closed her eyes and the comforting weight of Will's strong arm had settled around her shoulders. Rather than unsettling her, the protective strength of his gentle hold had eased her fears and his supportive touch had stayed with her all night.

I'm not afraid when I'm with you.

Her heart skipped a beat as she recalled her words from yesterday. She couldn't believe she'd uttered them out loud, but they were just as true today.

Being around Will felt completely different than the time she'd spent with Preston.

With Preston, she'd tiptoed around him in person and in conversation, always afraid to do or say something that would ignite his temper. Each morning, she'd choked back her fear, poured his coffee and prepared his breakfast with a steady hand, her fingers cramping for an hour afterward from the strain of fighting off nervous tremors to avoid spilling anything and setting off his temper. And each night, she'd pulled back the top sheet—the clean white sateen set Preston liked—and lain stiffly in bed, waiting and wondering, always wondering through the long dark hours, if his attention would turn to her…and how badly his touch might hurt.

In all the years she'd lived with Preston, she couldn't recall a single night she'd slept peacefully. But last night, in Will's arms, on damp ground in the middle of backcountry, she'd slept more deeply and soundly than she ever had before.

Will's lips parted and a soft sound escaped him.

Taylor sat quietly for a minute, and when he didn't awaken, she eased out of the lean-to and moved away quietly, strolling across the meadow. Tall grass, beaded with dew, brushed her shins and tickled her knees. Disturbed by her steps, two butterflies fluttered up from the thick grass and flew away, their colorful wings silhouetted against the golden sun rising in the distance, peeking over the mountain range.

Stopping at the edge of the meadow, she hugged her arms across her chest and blinked away the last lingering dregs of sleep as she watched the sun's bright glow spread slowly across the sky. Her muscles ached, her throat was parched—all things considered, she should feel pretty ragged by now.

But she didn't.

She grinned, tipped her chin up and savored the gentle warmth of the sun's rays. The higher the sun rose, the more the sky lit up with color. Pink, lavender and purple streaked in all directions, creating a stark contrast with the white mist hovering low along the mountain range.

"You trying to tell me something?" she whispered softly, her gaze drifting over the spectacular sky above her. "Because I'm ready to listen now. I'm ready to do my part."

That small feeling that had stirred within her yesterday grew a little bit more. It streamed through her veins, warmed her skin the night air had cooled and lifted her chin higher.

You're an amazing woman, Taylor Holt. I hope you know that.

A twinge of regret returned, drawing her spirit down, and her vision blurred. A hot tear rolled over her cheek and settled in the corner of her mouth. She licked it away, the salty taste lingering on her tongue.

Preston had taken so much from her. She'd given him so much. Much more than she'd realized. And somewhere along the line, sometime during the years she'd spent with him, she'd lost her strength and her faith. She'd lost the person God had meant her to be.

I can be a better person, she prayed silently. *I can be who You meant for me to be. Who Will thinks I am.*

Or, at least, she hoped so. She looked down and twisted the toe of her shoe in the grass, her shoulders sagging. It was an easy thought. An easy dream. But it was a much harder accomplishment to bring to fruition in reality…especially when she was on her own.

A high-pitched call rang out and a broad-winged hawk flew overhead, coasted on the morning breeze along the tree line and circled over the thick forest beyond the meadow.

Taylor wiped her face, studied the mesmerizing sunrise once more, then glanced back at Will. He still slept, propped upright against the wall of the lean-to, head to the side, his chin resting on his shoulder.

They'd both been exhausted last night, and if his muscles had been as overworked as hers yesterday, he'd wake up to a stiff back and sore arms and legs.

Her stomach growled and she rubbed her belly, smiling absently. He'd probably be starving, too. She looked around and her gaze settled on a thick swath of bushes near the edge of the meadow, butting up against the forest. Clumps of red were visible, low among the leaves. Wild strawberries, probably. Same as the ones they'd found yesterday morning and apparently plentiful in the immediate area.

She shivered slightly and hugged her arms tight across her chest. Bears were plentiful around this area, too, according to Will. Bears like the ones they'd encountered yesterday, ones that had stalked them like prey and seemed pretty agreeable to taking berries off the menu and putting her and Will on it instead.

Taylor glanced at Will, then the forest, and back again. Well, it couldn't be helped. She was hungry, Will would be hungry when he woke, and they both needed some form of energy to hike the miles they were bound to face on their journey upriver today.

She inhaled, rubbed her shaky palms together and set her shoulders. Berries it was, then. And the sooner she tackled that pile of bushes, the better. With any luck...and maybe a little of God's help, the bears would sleep in this morning and she'd finish picking what she needed before they started roaming.

Please, Lord, she prayed silently. *Keep the bears at bay.* A bear encounter certainly wasn't the best way she could think of to start the day.

Over the next half hour, she picked through the thick bushes, plucked wild strawberries from their stems and gently piled them in the pouch she'd created in her

T-shirt by folding up the hem. Branches cracked and rustled several times in the distance, setting her nerves on edge and causing her to freeze in place, but luckily, in each instance, the culprit turned out to be a frisky squirrel or hungry chipmunk.

Still, she didn't care to take any chances, so she picked up the pace, collected another handful of berries in a hurry and kept scanning the forest in front of her, peering deep into the dark areas in the distance where dense trees choked out the light of the sun.

"Breakfast as usual?"

Taylor squealed and spun around, her hands lifting in front of her and the hem of her shirt unrolling, the berries tumbling to the ground.

"Sorry." Will raised his hands, palms out, and grimaced. "Didn't mean to startle you."

Sighing, she pressed her hand to her chest, her heart pounding beneath her palm. "Well, you did. I thought you were a bear."

His lips twitched and one dark brow rose. "Bears talk?"

Oh, boy. No doubt he was handsome, but first thing in the morning—his thick hair tousled, strong jaw lined with dark stubble and a teasing grin on his face—he was downright irresistible.

Biting back a smile, she narrowed her eyes. "This thing you're doing right now—" she wagged her pointer finger at the soft curves of his mouth "—is it sarcasm? 'Cause it's kinda hard for me to appreciate it at the moment, seeing as how we were almost eaten yesterday doing exactly what I was doing when you snuck up on me."

He shook his head, his smile growing. "Oh, I didn't sneak."

She poked her finger at his chest. "You snuck."

"All right." He laughed and covered her hand at his chest with his own, his thumb stroking the back of her wrist softly. "Maybe I did sneak, but I didn't mean to, and I promise I won't do it again." His dark head lowered and his lips brushed her knuckles softly. Then his brown eyes met hers again as he teased, "And I promise to save the sarcasm for a more appropriate place and time."

She bit her lip, the gentle touch of his mouth against her skin dancing over her wrist, up her arm and slipping dangerously close to her heart. "A m-more appropriate place and time?"

"Yeah." The teasing light in his eyes faded and a warm, hopeful expression took its place. "After this is over. When we get out of here."

He wanted to see her again. Another time, another place. After all of this? Her mouth parted, but words wouldn't emerge. That sweet tingling he'd stirred within her settled deep in her chest, stealing her breath.

The hopeful look in his eyes receded and a rueful expression appeared. "I didn't mean to overstep just now or make you uncomfortable. I just—"

"No. I…" She took a deep breath. Savored the excitement running through her, the pleasant trembling in her limbs so different than the kind of feelings Preston had always evoked in her. “I’d like that.” She smiled. “Very much.”

He smiled back. “I was hoping you’d say that.” Clearing his throat, he glanced down at their feet and a laugh escaped him. “Sorry about spilling breakfast.” He squeezed her hand, then squatted, picked up a strawberry and dusted it off. “I’ll round the berries back up if you’d like to rest in the lean-to again before we head upriver.”

“No, thank you.” Taylor knelt beside him, placed her hand on his warm forearm and met his eyes, her heart turning over in her chest. “We’ll pick them up together, then eat while the sun finishes rising. By then it’ll be time for us to head out.”

That charming grin returned, and before they began gathering the strawberries, Will repeated softly in the same gentle tone from last night, “Together.”

Will kept a steady pace up the winding riverbank, slowing his steps a bit to keep by Taylor’s side and avoid overtaxing her slightly slower gait. After the sun had fully risen, they’d finished off the last few berries, then hiked back to the riverbank and renewed their journey upriver, scanning the thick woods around them for any sign of Andi.

“Andi!” He listened carefully, studied the woods, rocks and river surrounding them, but only the sporadic chirp of birds, rustle of small animals in the trees and steady rush of the rapids met his ears.

There was no answering call and no sign of Andi.

A slow burn of restless energy coiled in his middle

and his legs strained to break into a sprint, wanting so badly to race up the steady incline of dirt and rocks, round each tree-lined curve and scream her name. But that wouldn't be wise.

For one, his mind was in better shape than his body. The little bit of juice he and Taylor had gleaned from their breakfast of wild strawberries hadn't gone very far in rehydrating them, and his gut still growled on an angry demand for food. His muscles were weak, there was no way of knowing how far they'd have to hike to reach Andi, and it wouldn't be long before the taxing demands of the past three days took their toll.

Better to conserve his energy…and help Taylor conserve hers.

He glanced to his right, his gaze trailing over her flushed cheeks, bright eyes and determined expression. Her pink lips parted on swift breaths as they approached a rocky incline and admiration flooded through him at the thought of all she'd sacrificed so far for Andi…and for him. For two people who were perfect strangers to her only four days ago.

Will lifted his hand, his fingers grazing the soft skin of her forearm before curling loosely around her elbow. "Careful here." He pointed to a trail of stones that glistened beneath the morning sunlight. "There's a wet stretch near the bend in the rapids. It'll be easy to fall. You can go first if you like, and I'll follow close behind. That way if one of us slips, maybe we can manage to hold each other up."

Those beautiful eyes of hers looked up at him, a

warm look of gratitude momentarily breaking past the shadow of exhaustion lining her features. "Thank you."

It'd be so easy to dismiss his concern for her as residual appreciation for the way she'd saved Andi from drowning, her ceaseless determination to accompany him on his journey to find Andi despite the dangers they faced and, most especially, the quiet words of encouragement she'd shared with him last night, calming his tirade against the unfairness of their situation and reminding him of his own sentiments that God still answered prayers even in the most difficult of times.

But that wasn't the whole truth. The strong and unexpected connection he felt for Taylor ran deeper than that, and he couldn't help but feel a strong surge of guilt. His focus should be on Andi right now. Not on Taylor, and especially not on pursuing any form of future with her.

Only...after hearing the hopeful but uncertain note in her voice last night as she'd questioned if God might be helping them even now—well, maybe this was part of that answer, too. Maybe there was a reason God had dropped him in the middle of backcountry with Taylor and not someone else. Because he couldn't resist embracing this newfound sensation of support she provided him. The kind of gentle companionship she'd offered him last night that had eased his worries and lightened his burdens. And a small voice inside him kept urging him to stick by her side to see where these feelings would take him.

"How far have we come?"

Will blinked and gripped Taylor's elbow tighter as she carefully stepped onto another wet stone. "What?"

"Miles." She glanced back at him, a concerned look passing over her face. "How many do you think we've covered so far?"

He stilled on the slippery rocks and shook his head, then glanced back at the rough terrain and up at the position of the sun, mentally calculating their progress. "Two miles? Maybe two and a half?"

She nodded, a shadow of exhaustion entering her expression. "I can see a smooth boulder just up around the bend, past the trees. Do you mind if we rest there for a few minutes?"

Yes, he did. All he wanted right now was to press on. To keep pushing with all he had to scale the next mountain and cover another mile. Anything to increase his chances of reaching Andi sooner.

"Sure," he said softly anyway, noting the slight breathlessness in her voice and slump of her shoulders. "As long as you'd like."

They pushed on, slowly stepping over deep crevices between wet stones, rounded the river bend and made their way to a smooth boulder near a set of rapids. Taylor sought a sunny spot on the sloping rock and Will followed, sitting beside her with a heavy breath.

Sunlight cut through the high trees and poured over the riverbank, warming their overheated skin even more, but the light spray of water from the rapids kept them cool, the sheen of mist forming tiny droplets on their faces, necks and bare arms and legs.

"All this water," Will said, watching the sunlight

sparkle over the beads of water coating the back of his hands. “And we can’t drink it.”

“I know.” Taylor lifted her legs up a few inches and swept her hand over the sheen of moisture on her skin. A wry smile appeared. “It’s so clear and looks so fresh, it’s all I can do to keep from dunking my head in the river and gulping.”

He studied her face, her pretty features that had grown so familiar in such a small amount of time, and he caught himself wanting to lean against her. He wanted to dip his head, bury his face in the graceful curve of her neck and release the tears that burned at the backs of his eyes against her sun-kissed skin. To feel her arms curl around his shoulders and hug him close. To draw strength from her comforting presence.

“We could,” he said softly. “But then we might end up regretting it later.” A renewed surge of guilt assailed him as he thought of Andi being alone, with no one to share her fears or comfort her. He faced the river again instead, blinked hard against hot moisture brimming along his lashes and clenched his jaw. “Andi probably feels the same way right now. She’s probably dehydrated, exhausted and hurting, too.”

He stared as white water crashed along the bank, spraying his legs.

Taylor’s hand curled around his knee and squeezed gently. “Andi’s strong. Very strong.” Her shoulder nudged his. “If she takes after you as much as I think she does, she won’t give up easily. She’ll keep fighting.”

Will dragged his hand through his hair and tried, unsuccessfully, to voice agreement. Thing was, Andi couldn't be more headstrong if she tried. There was no telling what chances she'd taken or what reckless choices she'd made. Like most young adults he knew, she thought she was invincible.

"We're going to find her," Taylor said. "We won't stop looking until we do. No matter what."

He looked up then, his eyes searching hers, and nodded.

She gave an encouraging smile, but it slowly faded as her gaze moved past him, focusing on something beyond him in the distance. "I was wrong," she whispered.

He frowned, his throat tightening. "What do you mean?"

Slowly, her smile reemerged—full-blown and relieved. "Look." She pointed at an area over his left shoulder. "She found us first."

He spun around on the boulder, his eyes scanning the thick woods behind him, and there was a small figure with an oversize dry bag slung over her shoulder, shoving through low-hanging branches and limping out onto the bank.

"Andi!" Will sprang to his feet.

She froze, her head swiveling in his direction and her eyes focusing on his face. The dry bag fell from her shoulder and her expression crumpled. "Dad!"

He slipped twice over the rocky bank, almost breaking his neck as he ran toward Andi, but it was worth it when he finally reached her, wrapped his arms around her and hugged her tight.

She sagged in his embrace, slumping heavily against

him as sobs racked her small frame. "I th-thought I'd never find you. Didn't know if you had drow—" As her voice broke, her hands curled around his neck, then patted over his shoulders and chest before lifting to cup his face, her thumbs rubbing over the thick stubble lining his jaw. Her relief was almost palpable as she searched for words, a dazed look in her eyes. "You… you look different. You're getting a beard."

A chuckle rumbled deep in his chest, then burst from his lips. Tears spilled over his lashes and poured over his cheeks. He smiled. "If it'll make you happy, I'll shave it the second we get home."

Andi shook her head, her breath catching on another sob. "No. Finding you makes me happy. Just seeing you. I didn't know if…" She buried her face against his chest and wrapped her arms around his waist—the same way she used to when she was a little girl. "I love you, Daddy."

Immediately, he hugged her tight and kissed the top of her head. He breathed her in, the scent of rain, soil and pine lingering in her hair. "I love you, too," he whispered, his voice catching as he savored the moment.

It felt like a lifetime since he'd been able to hold her close, safe and protected, without her pulling away. For the first time in years, Andi had met him halfway.

Chapter Nine

How could Heather have left them?

Taylor ducked her head and wiped away a tear as she watched Will hug Andi close, tuck her head beneath his chin and kiss her hair. How could a mother ever abandon her daughter? And how could Will's wife leave and put him behind her for years with no regrets at all?

"Are you hurt?" Will's deep voice vibrated with emotion as he skimmed his hands over his daughter's shoulders and arms, then tipped her chin up and inspected her face.

Andi looked up at him, an expression of relief appearing. "Just my ankle. But it's not too bad."

Will knelt in front of her and tapped her left leg. "This one?"

"No. The other." As Will gently probed Andi's right ankle to ascertain the injury, she glanced across the riverbank at Taylor and a hopeful eagerness lit up her face. "You're okay?"

Taylor nodded. "Thanks to your dad. He pulled me out of the river. Basically saved my life."

"We saved each other," Will clarified, cradling Andi's ankle with both hands. "Taylor saved me as much as I saved her." He glanced at Taylor, his eyes roving slowly over her face. "Kept us going last night, too. I was losing hope, but she reminded me it was worth it to keep going."

Andi's smile trembled and her eyes filled with a fresh onslaught of tears. She reached down and squeezed Will's shoulder, then hobbled past him on her left leg, crossing the rocky bank until she reached Taylor. "Thank you."

Andi threw her arms around Taylor, making her catch her breath in surprise. The young girl pressed her cheek to Taylor's shoulder and cried softly.

"I'm so sorry," Andi whispered brokenly. "I didn't mean to hurt you when you helped me in the rapids. I didn't mean t—"

"Shh," Taylor soothed, her heart breaking at the desperation in Andi's voice. "You don't need to apologize." She smoothed her hand over Andi's back as it trembled and added, "You didn't do anything wrong. Not a thing."

Andi shook harder in her arms. "I should've listened to Dad when he said it was too dangerous to go downriver. I shouldn't have made everyone get back in the water. Jax, Ms. Beth and Mr. Martin fell in the river and I don't know if they made it out. I looked for them while I walked downriver, but I didn't see them. What if they didn't make it?"

"Hey, now." Will crossed the bank and reached their side. "There's every reason to hope they're safe and well right now." He drifted his hand over Andi's hair as she cried in Taylor's arms. "And you're not responsible for what happened. We all made a decision together as a group, and the majority of the group chose of their own volition to proceed downriver. Myself included." He glanced at Taylor, a tired but teasing grin on his face, and winked. "Although I'll remind you both that I was the only one wise enough to dissent."

Oh, boy. There was that charm again. It was more than enough to make a woman weak in the knees where he was concerned.

Taylor waited a moment for the pleasant flutter in her chest to subside, then lowered her head until her mouth was level with Andi's ear and whispered, "As much as I hate to admit it, your dad is right."

Andi's sobs slowed and she lifted her head from Taylor's shoulder, her wide brown eyes moving from Taylor's grin to Will's. She bit her lip, then grinned, as well, her tears ceasing and a laugh escaping her. "I hate admitting it, too."

"Good," Taylor declared. "I'm glad I'm not the only one. And from now on, we'll have to work extra hard at keeping his ego in check."

She laughed harder, stepped back and wiped her face with the back of her hand.

Will kissed Andi's cheek, then mouthed *Thank you* at Taylor over Andi's head.

Cheeks heating, Taylor hid her blush of pleasure and gestured toward the dry bag Andi had dropped near the tree line. "That's a huge dry bag you hauled downriver with you, Andi. Please tell me it's the one Jax packed with bottled water."

Brown eyes sparkling with relief and excitement, Andi grabbed the dry bag. "Yep. It is. And there are iodine tablets, too, so when the bottled water runs out, we'll have a way to sanitize the river water. I found it stuck along the bank when I was walking downriver. Never found the rest of them, though."

"That's okay," Will said. "One dry bag's more than Taylor and I had a few minutes ago. And there are probably other things we can use in it."

For the next few minutes, Will dug through the dry bag and handed Taylor everything he found that might be of use. In addition to six bottles of filtered water and the iodine tablets Andi had mentioned, there were neutralizing tablets, as well, that would help provide cleaner, fresher-tasting river water after they'd purified it. All things considered, Taylor considered this a luxury.

A flashlight, blanket, cargo net, lighter, waterproof matches, two small towels and one plastic sandwich bag filled with six granola bars—one treat for each member of the group, courtesy of Jax, Will guessed—were also found.

Three bottled waters were guzzled down first. Taylor forced herself to slow down as she drank, sipping rather than gulping, and savoring the moist feel of the water in her mouth. The liquid provided relief for her dry, chapped lips, too, and she poured a little water in her cupped palm and splashed it on her sweaty face, almost sighing with pleasure.

"Oh, I'd kill for a bar of soap and bottle of shampoo right now," she groaned.

"Don't have any soap or shampoo," Andi said around a mouthful of granola bar. "But I found the campsite Jax talked about half a mile upriver—" she took another bite of granola and chewed "—and there's a cool swimming hole not far from it. A decent fishing hole, too."

"Andi." Will, grinning, eyed his daughter over the bottle of water he held near his lips. "Please chew and swallow first. Then talk. Being in backcountry is no excuse for neglecting your manners, especially when we're in the presence of a guest."

"Oh," she garbled. Face reddening, she chewed slowly, swallowed hard, then continued. "I know how to get back there if y'all want to go?"

Taylor glanced at Will, who raised a questioning eyebrow.

"What d'ya say, Taylor?" he asked. "You up for hiking another half mile today?"

She nodded eagerly. "If it involves a prepped campsite, a cool swim to wash the grime off and a chance at eating something other than berries and granola, I'm all for it."

Will drained the last drops of water from his bottle, then motioned toward the river. "Let's fill these empties, drop in a few iodine tablets and repack 'em. By the time we get ready to settle tonight, they should be purified."

They did as Will suggested, repacked the dry bag and headed through the tree line back upriver with Andi leading the way. It was slow going and Will insisted that they stop several times along the way so Andi could sit, prop her injured ankle up on a log or rock and rest. She argued good-naturedly with him each time, but the look of sheer relief that crossed her face when she sank onto the ground made it evident that she needed the rest breaks—probably more than she was taking, but Taylor could tell Will didn't want to push his luck and risk ruining the peaceful truce he and his daughter seemed to have reached.

Half a mile upriver, the thick tree line parted, a clearing emerged and a deep, cool mountain stream glistened in the late-afternoon sun. The roar of the rapids could still be heard over the trees, but an area of bare dirt near the stream remained relatively peaceful, and there was a perfect spot to build a fire.

Taylor sighed. If only the trip had gone as Jax had planned. She had no doubt the entire group would've spent the past two nights relaxing by the fire and enjoying each other's company. As it was, they were still stranded in the middle of nowhere without knowing if a rescue party would come or if they'd be able to hike their way out of backcountry. But then again, had the trip gone as planned…she never would've spent the past two nights with Will. And now that they'd found Andi safe and sound, she couldn't help but look back on the time they'd spent together with gratitude. Neither she nor Will had spent those nights alone. Instead, they'd had each other to lean on.

She dragged her foot across the ground, watching as blades of grass bent in passing, then slowly rose. Being able to trust and depend on a man was definitely a first. She was grateful she'd had the opportunity to experience that with Will. And…she found herself longing to hold on to that feeling. To hold on to Will.

"Taylor?"

She jerked around to find Will studying her closely. "I'm sorry—what did you say?"

"I asked if you wanted to take a dip in the stream, or if you'd rather rest first." He narrowed his eyes, concern crossing his face. "You okay?"

Andi squealed and a splash quickly followed. "It's chilly!" she called from the water, laughing. "Come on in, Dad."

Taylor glanced at the stream and smiled as Andi beckoned Will with a wave of her hand, then floated on her back, her arms sweeping slowly by her sides against the gentle current.

"Oh, I'm fine," Taylor said, slipping her hand under her shirt and ensuring the straps of her swimsuit were secure on her shoulders. Satisfied, she grabbed the mud-stained hem of her T-shirt, whipped it over her head, then grinned. "And I bet you ten to one that I hit the water before you do."

Will's mouth twitched. "You're on."

She toed her shoes off while he kicked his own off, then tugged his shirt over his head and tossed it on the ground. Then he held out his hand.

"May the best man win," he teased.

"May the best woman win," she countered. Ignoring

his hand, she shoved his bare chest with both hands, laughed as he stumbled back with a look of surprise, then raced toward the water.

His powerful steps followed quickly in pursuit, the feel of him at her back spurring her on. At the bank, she jumped and plunged feetfirst into the deepest stretch of the water, her head submerging just as he splashed in beside her.

Cool water washed over her skin, flowed with delicious ease through her grimy hair and provided a refreshing chill when she kicked to the surface and her head emerged again. After scaling a wall, being caked in mud and having tumbled through rapids twice, it was a gift straight from heaven. Ah, wonderful!

Water splashed in her face, stinging her nose.

"You cheated." The deep rumble of Will's soothing voice drew closer and moved around her in a slow circle, punctuated with splashes. "Your actions officially disqualify you from the race, and I win by default."

Taylor laughed and wiped her face, blinking water droplets from her lashes furiously until his handsome face came into focus in front of her. "Nope. That was a fair head start. You're at least a foot taller than me and that evened things up as they should be."

Will grinned, his muscular arms moving in circular motions as he treaded water next to her. "Hmm. I might give you a pass on that." He glanced at Andi, who no longer floated on her back but treaded water several feet away, watching them silently. "What's the verdict, Andi? Did Taylor win?"

Andi's brown eyes, a wounded light in them, left

Will and she stared at Taylor. A pensive expression overcame the half smile that faded from her face. "No. I was here first."

Will waded farther out to the middle of a calm stretch of the stream near the campsite, grabbed a smooth stone from the riverbed and stacked it on top of the small pile he and Andi had created to form a small dam to trap fish. Three feet to his left, stones clinked, and he glanced over, watching as Andi hefted a large stone on top of the emerging wall. She knew the drill; they'd gone through these motions at least a dozen times during her childhood years when they'd camped frequently on the weekends.

At the time, he'd suggested they fish using the survival technique for fun—thinking it'd end up being a novelty of sorts—but now, considering their present circumstances, he was grateful he'd started the tradition.

"You wanna tell me about earlier?" he asked, retrieving two more stones. He carried them over and placed them on the pile.

Andi fished another rock out of the water, added it to the wall of the small dam and lifted a dark eyebrow. "What about earlier?" she asked blandly.

"You know what. That stunt you pulled with Taylor." He jerked his thumb at one fully formed wall of the low dam they'd built. "And sit down and elevate that ankle before you strain it so badly you can't hike tomorrow."

She released a long-suffering sigh, limped onto the

grassy bank, plopped down and propped her right heel on a rock. "I don't know what you're talking about."

Stifling a groan of frustration, Will shook his head and tackled a new section of the stream, gathering up an armload of stones and carrying them over to the unfinished section of the dam.

An hour earlier, he could've sworn things were looking up. But less than two minutes after he and Taylor had plunged into the deep end of the stream, Andi's good mood had vanished. When he'd asked who'd won his and Taylor's race to the stream, Andi had shot him and Taylor both a dirty look, given a tight-lipped response, then limped back out of the stream, claiming she was too tired to swim.

Her supposed "rest" had lasted all of ten minutes, until the moment he and Taylor had finished their swim, dried off as much as possible with the small towels from the dry bag and redonned their clothing over their swimsuits. As soon as he'd invited Taylor to walk to the shallow end of the stream and help build a dam to catch fish, Andi had sprung up from her supine position on the grass, hitched her injured leg up and literally hopped on one foot to reach him faster, insisting she would be a better assistant.

Not willing to reject Andi's voluntary offer of help—something that hadn't occurred in over five years—he'd accepted. Taylor, fidgeting with her shorts and avoiding his eyes, had quickly agreed it was a good idea and announced she'd stay behind at camp and build a fire.

Having Andi by his side again lifted his spirits, no

doubt. But walking away from Taylor, especially after glimpsing a look of awkward discomfort on her face, dragged his good mood right back down again.

"What's bugging you, Andi?" he asked, filling in the last opening of the small dam.

"Nothing's bugging me."

"Then why were you so rude to Taylor?"

"I wasn't rude."

"Yeah, you were."

"Is that how you interpreted it?"

"There was no need for either of us to interpret it." Will spread his hands and raised his shoulders. "Your tone tipped us off."

Her mouth tightened. "So there's an *us* now? As in you and Taylor?"

Will dropped his head back and heaved out a sigh. *Lord, this one's Yours. You made her.* "You gotta be kidding me..." He inhaled a slow breath and tried again. "You see anyone else out here, Andi? It's just you, me and her."

Her nose wrinkled. "I'm well aware of that."

"And your attitude." Will grimaced. "Believe me, that right there is a whole other entity."

Hurt flashed in her eyes and her chin trembled. She turned away, staring at the rugged mountain range to the left of them.

"Andi..." Will took one step toward her, but when she stiffened, he stepped over the dam and grabbed the cargo net he'd pulled from the dry bag. "I can't make things right if you don't tell me what's wrong." He unrolled the net, stretched it out, then grabbed one end and hung it on a stick he'd wedged between two rocks on one end of the dam. "I'm only trying to help, you know? I'm doing my best here."

He'd always done his best. Problem was, his best didn't seem to be good enough anymore. Hadn't been for at least a decade.

Flinching, he picked up the other end of the net and stretched it across the opening between the dam walls, then threaded a second stick through it on the other side. He pulled it tight, creating a snug dead end in the middle of the shallow stream, and secured it to the riverbed by placing several heavy stones on the lower edge. Water gurgled through the netting easily, and after a patient wait, he should be able to wade in and scoop out at least three bass if he kept his hands slow and controlled.

Satisfied with the trap, he joined Andi on the bank, sat beside her and propped his elbows on his bent knees. They sat silently for several minutes, the only sounds the gurgling water, whispering buzz of bugs as they flew over the stream and a steady chirp of crickets in the thick woods along the opposite side of the bank.

Soon, the sun dipped in the sky, its lower half obscured by a distant mountain range, and a sharp ray of sunlight cut across the stream and spilled over Andi's face. Suspicious moisture gleamed in her eyes.

"Help me out, please," he said softly. "I don't understand."

She continued staring straight ahead, then parted her lips and said in such low tones he had to lean closer to hear, "It's always been just us."

"Yeah." Of course. For more than a decade. Nothing new there. "I'm not following you."

"Just us." She faced him then, tears welling on her bottom lashes. "But now she's here."

"I thought you liked Taylor. Just a few days ago you were siding with her against me."

"That was before."

He huffed out an exasperated breath. "Before what?"

"Before you spent two days alone with her," she said slowly. "Then became an *us* with her. Without me."

Oh, man. She was jealous. This was definitely a new argument. How in the world had he not seen this one coming? And how should he navigate it?

"None of the three of us ended up where we were three days ago because we had a choice in the matter," he pointed out gently. "I didn't choose to be separated from you. I'd never choose that, Andi."

One fat tear spilled over her lashes and rolled down her left cheek. "You promise?"

"I promise." He lifted his hand and gently wiped the tear away with his thumb. "The only reason I came out here at all was to spend time with you. To take whatever time you'd give me. I miss you. I've been missing you for the past several years. More than you'll ever know."

Confusion suffused her features. "I've been right there at home all the time."

"No, you haven't."

Her shoulders sagged. "I only took off the once. And I didn't do it to hurt you or scare y—"

"I know." A breeze sifted through the trees and

swept over them. He smoothed an errant hair from her forehead. "But it hurt me just the same. I was terrified."

She looked at him in surprise.

"Yep." Throat tightening, he turned his head and watched the water stream through the net. "Dads get scared, too, you know? Especially when it comes to their daughters." He swallowed the tight knot in his throat. "For almost a week, I worried myself sick imagining what might have happened to you out there on your own. You didn't call—not once. Wouldn't answer any of my calls or respond to my text messages, either." He hesitated, but considering this might be his only opportunity to make his point, he forced himself to forge ahead. "How did you feel when you couldn't find me two days ago?"

Her face paled. "Awful."

"You were afraid for me?"

She stared at the ground and nodded.

He drew in a deep breath. Steadied his voice. "Multiply that fear by ten and add five more days to the duration. That's how I felt when you ran away two months ago."

Her head dipped farther down and she bit her lip.

"Where did you go?" he asked. "I know you don't want to tell me, but I got no place to go right now and I'm sticking to your side till you give it up."

At first, he didn't think she'd speak. It occurred to him that she might refuse to ever tell him, just like the dozens of times over the past two months when he'd asked the same question. And he might never find out what she did the week she disappeared. But then…

"I went to Nashville to see Mom."

His spine stiffened and he studied her face, looking for any twinge of pain, hoping not to find it. But it was there, flooding her eyes, and he didn't have to ask. He knew the answer. "You found her."

Another nod. Her voice shook. "I looked her up. Found her online. Did you know she sings in a club?"

"Yes."

"I wasn't old enough to get in," she continued. "So I followed her home."

He took a moment to collect himself. "What happened?"

"She recognized me. She knew who I was without me telling her." She faced him, her eyes clinging to his. "Did you send her pictures of me? You told her I wanted to see her?"

Reluctantly, he dipped his head. "I send her a photo every year on your birthday and I let her know you still ask about her. I told her I'd welcome her, if she ever wanted to stop by to visit you. That I wouldn't turn her away so long as she was willing to do right by you. I never told you because I didn't know how she'd react. And I didn't want you to get your hopes up, then get hurt if she didn't show."

Her voice faded to a pained whisper. "She doesn't want me. Never will."

Anger lanced through his heart so badly he clenched his teeth to resist shouting. Instead, he wrapped his arms around her and pulled her close, tucking her into his side and pressing his cheek to the top of her head. "You're wanted," he said fiercely. "Wanted and loved.

I'll never be able to tell you how much. There aren't enough words for how much I love you. And it's her loss—*not* yours. I promise you that."

Andi curled her small fists in his shirt and buried her face in his chest, her next words breaking his heart into so many pieces he didn't think he'd ever be able to put them back together. "It doesn't feel that way."

She shook in his arms, her whole body trembling, and his shirt grew damp beneath her tears.

"I know, baby," he whispered painfully. "I know."

They sat by the stream for another hour and he held her while she cried, rocking her gently like he used to when she was a child, smoothing his hand over her hair and wishing he could lift the burden from her. Make it so she never hurt again.

His resentment for Heather intensified, and he tried his best to pray it away. Tried to appreciate the blessing God had given him recently in providing him an opportunity to get to know Taylor—a good, compassionate woman who he was sure would never knowingly hurt Andi or him the way Heather continued to do.

The thought of Taylor waiting for them back at the campsite, her warm smile and giving nature…the warm, supported way she made him feel—it brought him a great relief he'd never felt before. And his heart lightened a little at the prospect of what could potentially lie ahead. A second chance at a relationship, an opportunity for Andi to form a friendship with an honest woman who would respect her. And as for he and Taylor, maybe a friendship stronger than the one he'd only imagined he'd had with Heather. Something more. Maybe even in time…love?

Then Andi pleaded, "It's always been you and me, Dad. Promise it'll stay just us."

Chapter Ten

Taylor tossed another log onto the campfire she'd built and stepped back as it sparked and shot red-hot embers into the dusky sky. She looked up and smiled. The late-afternoon sun was only half an hour away from setting and splashed bold golden colors across the horizon. In the distance, along the darkest fringes of the sky in the opposite direction, two stars blinked down at her, and the surrounding trees, their tall tips cloaked in mist, pulsed with the rattle of cicadas.

She closed her eyes, swaying slightly to the chorus of the crackling fire, the whispering stream and throbbing sound of wildlife.

Those are His waters. His smoke.

And His mountains, Taylor added silently, recalling Jax's words. What was it Jax's pops used to say?

When the world broke a man, all he had to do was come to God's land and let Him know he's here. Peace is in this place—all around. You just got to look for it.

She hadn't believed it. Not then. But if she were honest with herself, she was beginning to. Having experienced such turmoil over the past few days, she'd never expected to find such a tranquil scene as this one and the elk from last night. But both moments had provided the same peaceful sense of security.

Twigs snapped several feet away and the low murmur of voices drifted in.

"Hey," Taylor called as Will's and Andi's figures emerged around the bend. "How'd it go? Are we having fish for supper?"

Andi didn't answer. She continued staring down at the ground as she walked, her shoulders stiff and hands shoved in the pockets of her shorts.

"Managed to snag five rock bass," Will answered, holding up a small pile of fish wrapped in the spare cargo net. "They're not the biggest in the world, but it's something other than granola and berries."

Taylor grinned. "That's enough to make me happy." She reached out and touched Andi's arm when she limped past. "Would you like to help me cook the fish? I rigged up a little grill of sorts. Piled some rocks right next to the fire, so we could spread them out and cook them faster."

Andi glanced up, her eyes red and slightly swollen. She opened her mouth to speak but stopped, glanced back at Will, then said, "Yes, please. Thank you."

Hesitating, Taylor met Will's eyes and raised a brow in question. He shook his head slightly, a sad smile emerging.

"Okay. Let's get supper started." Taylor gentled her tone and rubbed her hands together. "May I borrow your knife, Will? I thought we could clean 'em and gut 'em by the stream first."

He smiled—a real one this time. "You not afraid to get your nails dirty?"

She laughed and trailed a hand through the tangled strands of her hair. "Considering I'm carrying about half the backcountry in my hair, I don't think it'll really make that big a difference."

Will chuckled and Taylor thought she caught a hint of a smile forming on Andi's face, but it disappeared just as quickly as it emerged. There was a cloud of sadness hanging over both of them, but she couldn't decipher what it was, and considering she was little more than a stranger to Andi, she didn't feel comfortable asking the young girl.

So, she chose to lead the way to the stream instead. They hauled the fish to the stretch of water closest to the campsite and Taylor started scaling the fish. Will cut off the heads and Andi washed the gutted fillets in the stream, then stacked them in a neat little pile, and they returned to the campsite.

Taylor spread the fillets out on stones next to the flames and they sat around the fire silently for a few minutes, their gazes lingering on the spectacular sunset over the western mountain range, then drifting over the bright pulse of stars as they emerged in the dark velvet background of the eastern sky.

"It's an odd feeling," Taylor said quietly.

Will shifted next to her and she could feel his eyes on her face. "What is?"

Taylor gestured toward the sky. "Being caught between day and night. Sun and stars. Feels like you're in a limbo of sorts. Like things could go either way." She studied the sunset as it slowly faded away. "Before you came back, I remembered what Jax told us the first day when we were scouting the rapids. I have to admit, I'm beginning to believe him."

"What did he say?" Andi asked softly. She sat, legs crossed, on the opposite side of the fire, staring into the flames.

Taylor smiled. "That there's peace all around. You just have to look for it." The last of the sunlight receded and night fell, bringing the flames of the fire into stark relief against the darkened landscape, and more stars fought their way out of obscurity, shining brightly down at them. "He was right. It's beautiful."

A quiet sniffle emerged from Andi's direction.

Taylor frowned, her heart aching as the glow of the fire lit up the sad expression on Andi's face. "Andi, has your dad brought you out here before?"

She shook her head. "Not here. But we've been to plenty of places like it."

"When we used to camp, we stuck closer to home," Will added, easing closer to the fire. "There are several gorgeous campsites out our way, aren't there, Andi?"

She remained quiet for a moment, then smiled a little. "Yeah." She wiped her eyes with the back of her hand, then watched the flames of the fire flicker, a soft giggle escaping her. "I remember our trip to Badger's Crossing. We rode the rapids, then camped overnight." Her smile grew. "A skunk got in Dad's tent."

Will laughed and leaned back into his hands. "Took

me a week to get the stink off me. No matter how many showers I took or how long I scrubbed, I couldn't get rid of it."

Andi perked up a bit. "He made this weird mixture with baby shampoo to kill the stink and bathed with it for a week, so he smelled like an infant for days."

He winced. "I think we're wandering into the territory of overshare, Andi."

"And then there was the time when we ran across that wild boar on the trail," Andi continued. "It had its babies with it and went after Da—"

"I think the fish are ready." Will, his cheeks scarlet beneath two days' worth of dark stubble, dragged a hand over the back of his neck. "Who's ready to eat?"

Taylor grinned. "Don't change the subject. I was enjoying Andi's stories." She tipped her hand toward Andi. "Please continue."

Eyes brightening, she licked her lips, shot Will a look, then said, "One time, we went spelunking, and when a bat flapped around the cave, Dad ran so fast I almost couldn't keep u—"

"Okay," Will said, his whole face scarlet. "That's enough sharing for the night." He rubbed his hands together briskly and picked up one of three long sticks he'd placed by the fire. "Taylor, would you like the first fish?"

She bit back a laugh. "Wait a sec. You're afraid of bats?"

He cocked an eyebrow. "You telling me you aren't?"

"I didn't say that, but we're not talking about me

right now." Taylor raised her eyebrows in return. "So you're really afraid of bats?"

He blew out an exasperated breath. "Yes. All right? I'm terrified of them." An expression of revulsion crossed his face. "They have pointy ears, a pig nose and creepy feet." He shuddered. "We're not on good terms."

Taylor laughed louder, the thought of his muscular bulk taking off in a sprint at the mere flap of wings almost impossible to believe. Only…

"But that first night," she said, her laughter fading. "When we were stranded in the storm, you went inside that cave and told me to wait outside while you checked it out." She tilted her head as he met and held her gaze. "There could've been bats in there."

He dipped his head. "I suppose."

"But you went in anyway."

"Yeah."

"Why?"

His dark eyes left hers and drifted over her face. "For you."

A wave of affection surged through her chest. "For me?" she whispered.

"Yeah," he said softly. "You were hurt and afraid. There was a storm brewing and you needed shelter."

Her breath caught, those delicious emotions within her intensifying. With Preston, she'd always been afraid and he would never have put her comfort before his own. But the first day she'd met Will, he'd been willing to face one of his fears just to make her—a stranger at the time—safe and comfortable. He was a true…

"Gentleman," she said out loud, admiring the play of shadow and light from the fire over his wide shoulders, strong jaw and mesmerizing brown eyes. "You're a good man, Will."

A tender smile crossed his face, and sincerity entered his tone. "I only did what any decent person would do."

Her smile returned. "Unless you'd been alone. If you'd been by yourself, would you have gone in that cave?"

He laughed. "Probably not. I'd have rather risked getting hit by lightning." His laughter died abruptly. "You saved my daughter's life, and she's the most precious person in the world to me. If Andi had been with me, I'd have done the same for her." He drew his head back and glanced at Andi, his tone sobering. "We've always been a team, haven't we?"

Nodding, Andi stared back at him, relief shining in her eyes. "Yes. You and I are the best team."

And no one else is a part of that. Andi hadn't said the words, but her tone was clear.

Taylor gripped the log she sat on with both hands and rubbed her thumbs over the smooth wood absently. That was why Andi had been so short with her earlier today when they'd swum in the stream. She'd shared a close moment with Will, much as she had just now, and Andi had been threatened by it.

Taylor glanced at Andi, who smiled up at Will as he handed her a fish skewered on a stick, and her chest tightened at the sadness still lingering in her eyes. She looked down at the fire, regret moving through her as she watched orange embers pop, then scatter, mingling with gray smoke and drifting on the night breeze toward the stars.

The last thing she'd ever want to do was make Andi feel as though she were trying to pull Will away from her, but it seemed as though that was what Andi thought she had done. But even worse, the thought of pulling away from Will for Andi's sake, of not exploring the bond they'd begun to form—one that was strong and good—was as equally disturbing to her.

She'd never known a good man like Will before. Had never dreamed she'd ever begin to feel the way she did for him—

Wait. How did she feel about Will? She was attracted to him, sure. He was a handsome man. But it had grown into more than that. The feelings she'd begun to experience for Will were warm and tender and tugged strongly at her chest. It almost felt like… like falling in love.

Her breath caught at the realization, and when she glanced at him, when she met his eyes and felt that tender tug in her chest again, she knew without a doubt. At some point during their short journey through the backcountry, this strong, kind and considerate man had quickly ducked beneath her guard and slipped right into her heart. So quietly. So unexpectedly. And she was falling in love with him.

"Aren't you going to sleep, too?"

Will smoothed a stray hair off Andi's cheek after she lay down by the campfire and shook his head. "Not yet." He spread one of the towels from the dry bag over her—not the best blanket, but it would do in a pinch. "As tired as I am, I'm still too keyed up to sleep."

He was also too full of past regrets. Too worried about the present. And too fearful of what the future may hold.

Andi lifted her head and peeked around him at the grassy bank near the stream. "How long do you think she'll stay out there?"

Will glanced over his shoulder and studied Taylor's silhouette beneath the moonlight. She stood near the stretch of stream where they'd swum earlier that afternoon, her head tipped back, attention on the bright full moon and impressive expanse of stars glittering above them. The glistening night sky was so wide and encompassing it seemed to take on a life of its own, drawing closer with each passing hour and lowering like a sparkling curtain around them, hugging the mountain peaks and moving with the breeze.

Two hours earlier, as they'd sat by the fire, Taylor had grown quiet after their lighthearted exchange over their first night in the cave and had become increasingly withdrawn as they'd eaten fish. He and Andi had continued sharing anecdotes of past camping trips and reminisced over the good times they'd shared together years ago as the moon had slowly emerged, but as relieved as he was to find Andi opening up to him again—actually sharing her pain rather than hiding it—he couldn't shake the feeling that the more Andi embraced him, the more Taylor seemed to pull away. And when they'd finished eating an hour ago, Taylor had thanked him for the meal, excused herself and slipped quietly away while he and Andi had continued chatting by the fire.

"She's been out there by herself for so long," Andi added quietly.

Reluctantly, Will pried his attention away from Taylor and faced Andi again. "I think she's used to being alone. She mentioned that she doesn't have any family. That she was married once but that her husband passed away."

Andi, eyes heavy with sleep, blinked slowly as she looked at Taylor again. "What happened to him?"

"I don't know. Didn't seem appropriate to ask at the time."

"Does she have any children?"

"No." Will managed a small smile and squeezed her shoulder. "And having you is one of the blessings I've always been most grateful to God for. When your mom left, I had you."

His mind wandered back then, mulling over memories of sleepless nights, mixing formula at two in the morning, soothing cries, leaving for work at 5:00 a.m., putting in overtime, picking Andi up from daycare, then…starting it all over again.

It had been grueling, exhausting work. But there had been so many rewards—like that brief window of time between eight and nine at night when he'd soothed and settled Andi for the night. The grin that had always lifted Andi's rosy cheeks during her bath when he'd trickled warm water over her shampooed hair. The giggle that would burst from her toothless gums when he'd tickle the bottoms of her tiny toes, and the most precious moment—the one where she'd drift off to sleep in his arms, curled into a ball, her light weight snuggled happily against his chest. Right over his heart. Those moments drew away all the day's pain and filled him with fresh energy to tackle the next one.

Nothing in the world had ever been more valuable to him than that time spent with her.

"We always had each other," he added softly. "Neither of us were ever alone. I don't think Taylor's ever had that."

Andi's brown eyes studied his face, then drifted over to Taylor. "So she doesn't have anyone?"

Will shook his head. "Not that I know of." He nudged her chin gently with his knuckle. "That's why I always try to remember that everyone struggles with something, and sometimes my burdens pale in comparison with others'. No matter how much I may hurt, it's important to save room in my heart to help others when I can."

"That's why you went in the cave," she whispered slowly, her lashes lowering. "So she wouldn't be alone."

He lifted his hand, smoothed his thumb over her flushed cheek and pondered that. Yeah. That had been part of it. But even then, as early as that after meeting Taylor, something else had driven him. That small voice inside him had slowed his steps during their walk from the riverbank to the cave, kept his gaze moving back over his shoulder to check on Taylor's progress, to make sure she still held her own despite her injury. A silent pull on his mind and heart had kept his attention and concern on Taylor—a feeling of kinship. Familiarity.

It was as though his heart had always known her. As though he may have been waiting for her all this time without even knowing it.

"Maybe I did it for more reasons than that." He tensed and glanced down at Andi, the thought having escaped his lips before he realized he'd uttered it.

But she was asleep now. Soft breaths moved past her parted lips and her body almost sagged with exhaustion against the hard earth beneath her.

"Sleep well, angel." He bent, kissed her temple, then stood.

Taylor was still standing by the stream, her head tilted back toward the sky.

Will walked in her direction, then hesitated briefly, his shoes shuffling over dirt and grass as he glanced back at Andi's sleeping form, highlighted by the fire. Then he resumed walking until he reached Taylor's side.

She continued studying the sky, but her blue eyes darted his way once as he shoved his hands in his pockets, then shifted away and refocused on the stars.

"Find something interesting up there?" he asked softly.

A small smile tugged at the curves of her lips. "I hope so. That's where you told me to look."

His brow furrowed. "I did?"

She nodded and a light breeze whispered between them, ruffling her hair and trailing a blond strand over her graceful neck. His gaze lingered there.

"When we were scaling the wall," she said. "You told me to look up. You said, that's where we were headed."

He laughed. "Guess I was aiming too high, because we sure didn't reach the top of that bluff the next day."

She laughed, too, the gentle sound stirring a pleasurable sensation in his chest. "We tried at least. I think that's what matters."

"Yeah. I suppose you're right about that." He narrowed his eyes and peered in the distance, the bright, sprawling reach of moonlight and stars darkening the rugged landscape. "With any luck, that rescue chopper will swing back by either tomorrow or the next day. It'd help if we were on higher ground. Somewhere above all these woods and rocks." He gestured upriver, toward a high mountain peak. "If I remember right, about two miles that way, we passed an outcrop once we cleared that first set of rough rapids before the second set dumped us. It's a crag I'd guess to be about five thousand feet up or so. If there's someone out there looking for us, that'd be a good place to be seen. It's high and by the river, but we'd have to pass through a ravine to get there. We could head out first thing in the morning and should make it by midafternoon."

"And Andi?" she asked, glancing back at the fire. "Will she be able to hike that far and make the climb with her ankle the way it is?"

He looked at Andi, a sense of pride moving through him as he watched the firelight dance over her cheeks and arms. "She'll try. She made it all the way to us on her own. And if she gives out, I'll carry her the rest of the way."

"You never get tired, do you?" She looked at him then, admiration in her blue eyes as they roved over his face.

"I'm tired all the time," he admitted, his cheeks heating. "Some days I just go through the motions. Do whatever is needed to wrap things up at work, get home and check on Andi." He held her gaze, kept his voice soft. "I don't ever want her to feel like she's alone."

Taylor smiled up at him, a pained look of longing moving through her expression. "Andi's lucky to have you."

"Who did you have at her age?" He bit his lower lip, waiting for her answer, hoping he hadn't pushed too far.

"The staff at three children's shelters." She looked away, resumed staring at the stars. "Then two sets of foster parents. And two years after I aged out of the system, I had Preston."

"Your late husband?"

She nodded.

"Did you know your parents?"

"No. From what I was told, I was abandoned outside a hospital as an infant. There's no record of who my parents are."

"And Preston? How did you meet him?"

Her mouth tightened. "I found work as a secretary in a real-estate office in Nashville. I enjoyed it more than I expected. I think it was because I got to see so many newlyweds, families and retired couples find their dream homes. A place to love, laugh and rest. A haven." Despite her tense tone, she smiled. "That was the good part. The best part, actually. Getting to help people find that and seeing how wonderful it felt to have your dream fulfilled." Her smile faded. "I think that's why I was drawn to Preston. He was a real-estate agent—the best in the area—and he'd show me these beautiful homes, walk me through them, sell me the dream. He made me think I could have that. He made me believe that he and I could build that dream together."

"And did you?" Will asked quietly. "Build the dream?"

"No." Pain twisted her expression, her features highlighted by the moonlight. "He walled us inside a nightmare."

It hit him then. The panicked, fearful look in her eyes when he'd knelt over her by the riverbank two nights ago. The desperate way she'd scrambled back across the dirt away from his hands, his touch.

"He hurt you." Anger stiffened his tone and his hands clenched into fists inside his pockets.

"All he knew was pain," she whispered. "That's what his father taught him. What his grandmother taught his father. Pain and anger filled the house where he grew up, and he filled ours with it, too." Her chin trembled. "I thought maybe if I prayed hard enough… if I showed him a different way—a different kind of love—maybe he'd understand. Maybe he'd try to work through his past and embrace a better way of living. But he never did."

His throat tightened at the thought of what she'd

endured. "I'm sorry, Taylor. I can't imagine what that must've been like."

"Can't you?" Her gaze sought his, her look of certainty catching him by surprise. "Heather did the same, didn't she?"

He shook his head. "She never—"

"Scarred you on the outside," Taylor agreed. "But she scarred you here." She touched her chest, her fingertips resting over her heart. "She hit you and Andi where it would hurt the most, didn't she? Then took off and left you with the pain? Left you to deal with it alone?"

His eyes burned. He looked away and focused on the moon that glowed in the distance, just as Taylor had for so long, and swallowed hard against the knot that formed in his throat. "Yeah."

"Sometimes..." Her voice faded as she stared at the moon, too. "Sometimes I can't understand why He doesn't answer. Why He doesn't help us when we need Him so badly."

Will's vision blurred and he blinked hard, choking back his anger and shoving away his doubts. He pulled his fist from his pocket, unfurled his hand and covered Taylor's with his own. "But He's helping us now, isn't He? Just like you said He was by using the mudslide to get us to the other side of the river." He looked down at her, the hint of relief beginning to shine in her eyes, giving him hope. "And at the moment, neither one of us are alone."

A tear rolled down her flushed cheek and pooled

in the corner of her mouth. She turned her hand over, threaded her fingers through his and squeezed. “I’m trying to believe that.”

Chapter Eleven

Taylor folded a small towel and put it back in the dry bag that lay by the charred remnants of the previous night's campfire. "Did you sleep well last night?"

Andi, who sat on a log on the other side of the campfire and sipped purified water from one of the plastic bottles they'd filled yesterday, nodded slowly. "Yes. Thank you." She glanced at the nearby stream, where Will squatted on the bank, dunked his hands into the stream, then splashed water on his face. "Did Dad?" She frowned up at Taylor, an accusatory note in her tone. "And did you?"

Taylor wiped her hands on her shorts, knocking off the dust and grime from smothering the last smoldering dregs of the fire and cleaning up their small campsite. "Yes, he did. After you fell asleep, he stayed up a little longer and we talked for a bit. Then he lay beside you and slept soundly. I tried to doze, but I couldn't, so I stayed up and kept an eye on things for a while."

Until sunrise, actually. After Will had taken her

hand in his, they'd stood beneath the night sky together for almost an hour. They'd barely spoken after she'd shared a little of what she'd been through with Preston. Instead, they'd continued staring up at the moon, thinking, and—surprisingly enough, Taylor reflected—she'd prayed silently.

For years, her relationship with God had faltered, then faded. Some of it had been due to the increasing pain and fear in her marriage and some of it had arisen from the flood of doubt and disappointment that had taken root in her heart for so long. And the guilt…that was always there. Probably always would be.

"You didn't sleep at all?" Andi asked.

"I couldn't." Taylor shrugged. "But in a way, it was a good thing, because I was able to stay up and keep a lookout. It gave me peace of mind to know that you and your dad were safe while you slept."

Andi's brow furrowed as she contemplated that. She took another swig of water, then tipped the bottle Taylor's way. "There's not much water left. Would you like some?"

Taylor smiled. "No, thanks. After I help your dad pack up supplies, I planned to take the empties downstream a bit. When we were swimming, I noticed a spring running nearby and thought I'd pull us some water from there. We'll still need to purify it, but it might have a cleaner taste."

"What will have a cleaner taste?" Will, rubbing his wet hair with one of the small towels, walked across the grass and joined them by the extinguished campfire.

"Water from the spring downstream," Taylor said.

"Oh." A mocking expression of disappointment crossed his face as he teased, "Thought y'all were rustling up a five-course breakfast."

Taylor grinned. "Thinking about that rib-eye steak again?"

He laughed. "Not gonna lie. I might've dreamed of one a time or two last night."

Taylor laughed with him, took a moment to admire his boyish grin and teasing tone, then glanced at Andi, whose eyes moved from her to Will and back slowly. "Well," she said, "think I'll gather up the empties and head to the spring." She bent, dug around in the dry bag and pulled out two empty bottles. "I'll fill these and drop in some iodine. I saw a strip of brush nearby that'll probably be full of wild strawberries, and we'll need fuel for today's hike, so I'll pick a few handfuls of those, too, while I'm there." She smiled at Will. "When I get back, I'll help you pack u—"

He held up a hand. "No. I can take care of this."

"Then I'll help Taylor." Andi stood, brushed off the back of her shorts with one hand and held up the empty water bottle she held in the other. "I drank more water than both of you put together, so the least I can do is help fill the bottles back up."

Will's brows rose. He studied Andi for a few moments, then looked at Taylor. "That okay with you?"

Taylor nodded, a strange mix of apprehension and hope moving through her. "Of course." She smiled. "I'd love the help."

After collecting the empty water bottles, she and Andi made their way upstream toward the spring. An early-morning mist still floated over the stream and riverbank, but a slight chill lingered in the air about them, cooling their skin and chasing away the last bit of sleep still clinging to them. Taylor glanced around, eyeing the stream and surrounding woods, but all seemed calm and peaceful.

Relaxing, she inhaled a strong lungful of sweet, clean mountain air. "It really is beautiful out here."

Andi murmured an assent, still limping slightly from her injury. "Me and Dad used to do this all the time." A blush snaked down her neck. "Well…not exactly this. I mean, we've run a ton of rapids before, but we've never gotten stuck out in the middle of nowhere like this before. Usually it's a lot more fun."

Taylor grinned. "I knew what you meant. And I enjoyed your stories last night. It sounded like you and your dad used to take a lot of wonderful trips together."

"Yeah." She glanced over her shoulder at Will, who moved around the campsite, packing up supplies and cleaning up any scraps they'd left behind from last night. "I'm hoping we'll go on more of them now." She shrugged and a small laugh escaped her. "Except maybe the end result will be better."

Taylor nodded. "Now, that's a hope we can all get behind."

Andi's smile slipped and her steps slowed. "Do you…?" She glanced at Taylor under her lashes. "Do you think we'll make it out of here?"

Taylor slowed her pace to match Andi's. "I think so." She smiled gently. "Your dad's like you—intuitive and strong—and I believe he'll find a way to get us out of here safely. Matter of fact, that's what we're going to tackle today by hiking to the outcrop."

Andi's downfallen expression lifted a bit. "How long will that take?"

"Oh, a few hours or so. But considering what all of us have already been through, that'll be a breeze." She looked up, studied the splash of color from the morning sunrise as it spread across the clear sky. "Did you hear the helicopter two days ago?"

"Yeah. It was so far away, though."

"It flew over me and your dad at one point." When they reached the spring, Taylor stopped and gave Andi what she hoped was a look of confident encouragement. "It was right there. Close enough to see us if we'd just been on higher ground. Away from the trees. That's why we're going to the outcrop. We're going to climb to the top and flag it down the next time it passes."

Shadows of doubt crept into Andi's eyes. "Are you sure it'll come back?"

Taylor's heart melted at the wounded look of uncertainty on Andi's face. Andi had lived her entire life without a mother, and the loss had left so many unanswered questions and distrust in her life. Something Taylor understood all too well.

"I don't know." She lifted her hand, then hesitated, her hand hovering near Andi's temple for a brief moment before she slipped her fingers under the fall of Andi's brown hair and smoothed it back gently. "We'll pray about it, okay? And if nothing else, I know your dad will take care of you."

Andi stiffened, her eyes trained on Taylor's face,

then—in an almost unconscious gesture—leaned into her supportive touch. But it only lasted a second.

Abruptly, Andi pulled away and rubbed her temple, then limped toward a clump of bushes near the stream. "I'll get the berries," she said over her shoulder as she walked away.

Taylor sighed, watching as Andi bent and began poking through a thick bush in search of berries. Wouldn't do to push her too much or intrude on her space. And with the luck she'd had recently, Andi might interpret her offer of comfort as an opportunistic move to wedge herself between Andi and Will.

She proceeded to the spring, cleared several rocks out of the way, lined up the water bottles on the ground and began filling them one by one. Two bottles were filled, then a third, and she pulled a small pack of iodine pills from her pocket and added one into each bottle, then secured the top.

For a while, the steady snip of Andi picking berries, light gurgle of water into plastic bottles and chirp of birds filled the air. Then a soft rustling sounded nearby and a dark, familiar shape emerged from the tree line near the bushes where Andi stood.

Taylor froze, then straightened from the spring slowly and spoke softly. "Andi."

She didn't hear her. Instead, Andi bent lower, her brown hair swinging over her shoulder as she continued riffling through the bushes for more berries.

"Andi."

Finally, she looked up, confusion in her eyes as she surveyed Taylor. "What?"

"You need to stay calm and walk over here slowly." Taylor, eyes glued to the bear, watched as it roamed closer, nosing its way toward one of the bushes. "Drop the berries."

Frowning, Andi straightened and followed Taylor's gaze, her eyes widening as she noticed the black bear. "Taylor..."

Panic laced her voice.

"It's okay," Taylor soothed. "I'm right here. Just stay calm and walk toward me."

Body trembling, Taylor tried to slow the thoughts jumbling together in her mind. What had Will said? The "stay calm" part she remembered, but what else?

The bear raised his head, his bulky form bobbing slightly as his nose worked, sniffing the air, searching for the source.

What else had Will said? Stay calm, and don't... Don't what?

The bear stopped bobbing, lowered his head and locked eyes with Andi.

Oh, no...

"Taylor?" Andi's voice pitched and her hands dropped, scattering berries at her feet.

The bear grunted. Took one step toward Andi, then another. And another.

"Taylor!" Andi spun and took off, stumbling as her injured ankle failed to support her weight.

Don't run, Taylor recalled Will saying. *Stand your ground, shout him down and fight.*

"Don't run, Andi," Taylor shouted. "Don't r—"

The bear charged, his muscular bulk barreling

through the bushes, storming across the grass, chasing Andi as she fled.

Taylor snatched up two handfuls of rocks and ran toward them both, her shoes slipping and catching between stone crevices on the bank of the stream as she shouted, "No! Get out of here and leave her alone! Go!"

The bear continued its pursuit of Andi and gained ground, its heavy breaths rasping closer and closer.

Try to look bigger than he is. It's the only way to scare him off.

"Get out of here!" Taylor screamed and yelled, her voice choppy as she ran, gasping for air.

"Tayl—!"

The bear lunged, his paw swiping at Andi's back. Its claw caught her injured leg and jerked her off her feet. She hit the ground, her palms slamming onto the dirt to soften her fall, then scrambled wildly through the grass as the bear dragged her backward by her foot. A sharp scream burst from Andi, piercing the still morning air.

"Let her go!" Taylor ran faster, drew back her arm and slung a rock at the bear's head.

He flinched, growled deep in his chest, then rose up on his back legs and lunged over Andi toward her instead, his sharp claws extended.

She flung another rock, but it glanced off his broad shoulder and bounced harmlessly across the ground. His wet nose and massive head butted into Taylor's belly, knocking her off her feet. Her body slammed onto the ground, the impact stealing her breath.

There was a brief moment of stillness as a familiar

terror took hold, snaking through her, paralyzing her muscles, and she blinked at the clear sky above. Disjointed thoughts rushed through her mind, her attention latching on to one coherent thought that hissed through her as she recalled Preston's voice.

Don't move. Stay right there, and I'll come to you.

A low growl resumed, black fur brushed her exposed legs and a sharp claw dug into her thigh.

Galvanized with pain, anger and years of pent-up terror, Taylor shot upright, kicking and punching. Her feet hit thick fur and muscle, and her fists pounded soft tissue. Angry growls erupted from the bear, but she pressed on, lashing out and striking him until everything around her became an agonizing blur of blood, pain and anger.

Will double-checked supplies, ensured everything had been accounted for and packed them back into the dry bag. He'd just secured the bag when an ear-splintering scream pierced the air.

Andi.

He shot to his feet and ran in the direction of the sound, his heart hammering against his ribs as he peered ahead. There, dozens of yards ahead, running toward him, was Andi.

"Dad!" She tripped and stumbled, almost falling to the ground. Blood trailed over her shin and coated her injured ankle.

He met her halfway, catching her as her leg finally gave out. "What happened? Where's Taylor?"

Chest rising and falling on heavy sporadic breaths,

she motioned over her shoulder in the direction of the stream. "B-bear...has Taylor."

His hands clamped around her upper arms and he eased her to the ground. "Where?" She didn't answer. Her face paled and her teeth chattered. "Near the stream." She gulped in air. "By the bushes."

Will sprang up and ran again, forcing his legs to cover as much ground as possible while he scanned the area. And there, between the stream and a row of bushes, was Taylor, fighting off a black bear.

She was kneeling on the ground, legs and fists flailing, striking blow after blow on the bear's head and shoulders. Vicious growls and angry huffs echoed around the small clearing, just yards from where the stream peacefully flowed, creating a nightmarish contrast.

Throat closing, Will pumped his legs harder and waved his arms in the air. "Here! Over here!"

The bear jerked back, stepped away from Taylor and glared in his direction.

Will hustled faster, surging up the grassy slope in the bear's direction. "Get! Go on! Get out of here!"

Taylor was on her feet now, a large stick in her hands. She swung it at the bear and advanced toward the animal, hoarse shouts bursting from her lips. She swung a second time, then another. On the third swing, she landed a hard blow to the bear's eyes and nose.

Flinching, the bear reared backward, crashed through a line of bushes, then turned and ran, his black hide disappearing behind a thick swath of trees.

Taylor fell to her knees, heavy sobs escaping her as

she crumpled to the ground and lowered her forehead to the grass.

"Taylor?" Will drew to a halt beside her and touched his hand gently to her heaving back. She didn't answer—just continued sobbing. "He's gone now. You're safe now."

She curled closer to the ground.

"Is she okay?"

Will glanced over his shoulder and found Andi standing behind him, tears streaming down her face, balancing on her good leg. "I don't know," he whispered. "Taylor? If you're hurt, I need to see so I can help. Can you stand?"

Again, no answer.

Will crouched down, eased his arms beneath her and gently rolled her into his arms. Apart from a wound on her thigh, she looked relatively unharmed, as far as he could tell—which was a miracle in and of itself. He lifted her to his chest, then stood, the desperate cries racking her body, making his hands tremble. She buried her face against his neck, her hot tears rolling over his skin.

"Dad?" Andi dragged her forearm over her wet face, her tears drying but expression startled.

"It's all right," he said softly. "I think she's shook up, is all. Let's take her to the stream and help her rest a few minutes."

Andi shuffled around on her good leg and limped by Will's side as he carried Taylor over to the stream, eased her onto the bank and sat beside her.

Immediately, Taylor returned to his open arms,

pressed her cheek to his chest and gripped his T-shirt. "I—I killed him."

A wry smile twisted his lips. He smoothed his hand over her back and hugged her close. "Nah. You just gave him a scare, is all. That bear got off easy, all things considered."

She shook her head, her hair tickling his chin. "Preston."

His smile faded. "What'd you say?"

"Preston," she repeated, her voice hitching. "I killed him."

Will froze. "Your husband?"

He met Andi's shocked gaze over Taylor's head, then refocused on Taylor as she shook in his arms.

She was in shock. Confused. That was all. "Taylor." He leaned back, gently cupped her jaw and lifted her tearstained face from his chest. "What are you saying?"

She looked up at him, fresh tears flooding her blue eyes and dimpled chin trembling. "Five years ago, I…" Her voice broke and, sobbing, she continued. "Things got really bad. He attacked me almost every day over the smallest things." She shook her head. "No matter what I did—or didn't do—it would set him off. I knew if I didn't leave him, he'd end up killing me. I didn't want to believe that—I'd prayed so hard for God to change him—but I knew it was the truth. So I left him. I got an apartment and told him I wouldn't come back. That it was over." Tremors racked her body. "Things went okay for a month or so. Then he started calling. Started stopping by, asking me to change my mind. He apologized, begged for forgiveness. You know…" She looked away, her hair falling over her cheek, and tried to smile, but her lips twisted, shame engulfing her face. "Did the usual things I used to fall for."

Will smoothed her hair back, tucked it gently behind her ear.

"But I wouldn't give in," she continued. "One morning, I got dressed for work, went to the kitchen, poured a cup of coffee, and when I turned around, he was standing right there, watching me." She stared at the ground, an empty look entering her eyes. "He said, 'Don't move. Stay right there and I'll come to you.'" Her voice shook. "That's what he always said before he..."

Chest aching, Will cupped her cheek. "Before he'd hurt you?"

Taylor nodded, then whispered, her voice breaking, "Except that time he had a gun. And we fought." Her blue eyes met his again, shame flooding her features. "After I shot him, I tried to help him. I tried to make it right. But he said, 'You can't fix it now.' And he was right." Her expression crumpled. "I can't ever make it right. I can't take it back."

"Tayl—"

"He won't ever forgive me."

"Preston?"

"No. God." She stared up at him, blue eyes wide and voice breaking. "He won't ever forgive me, will He? For giving up on Him, or for what I did to Preston?"

Will studied her face. Watched her lips tremble and the dark shadows of despair return to her eyes. Reaching out, he cradled her face in his hands and drifted his thumbs through the tears streaming down her face. "He always forgives. All you need to do is ask."

A ragged breath left her as she stilled. "You believe that?"

"Yes," he whispered. "I do. I believe there's nothing we could ever do or not do that would cause Him to abandon us."

She continued peering up at him, her cries slowly subsiding.

"You did what you had to," he said softly. "Preston gave you no choice but to fight back. You're not a victim—you're a survivor. A strong, caring, wonderful woman who saved my daughter's life twice. And mine at least once." Emotion swelled in his chest, warm and pleasant, and streamed through his veins. "A woman I'm..."

He paused, his thumbs slowing to a stop on her flushed cheeks.

...falling in love with.

Face warming, Will glanced at Andi, the question in her eyes reflecting his own surprise at the strength of emotions running through him. He swallowed hard, set the overwhelming realization aside and refocused on Taylor's face.

"A woman I'm glad chose the same path as me and my daughter this weekend," he finished quietly.

Taylor's tears slowed. "I'm glad, too. Things may be rocky, but I'm very thankful I've had the chance to meet both of you. I just hope I didn't give you too hard a time the first couple of days."

A grin fought its way to his lips, the small action a

slight relief from the intense emotions swirling within him. “Nah. You’ve challenged me—kept me on my toes. I promise you this trip wouldn’t have been the same without you. I’d have been stranded on my own for two days with no one to brave the snake, mudslide and bears with.”

Andi scooted closer to them, a note of intrigue replacing the sad, fearful tone in her voice. “There was a snake? And a mudslide?”

Slowly, Taylor smiled back at him, tears drying on her cheeks as she glanced over at Andi. “There’s been a little bit of everything on this mountain.”

“And there’s more waiting on us,” Will said, his smile fading at the thought of Andi’s and Taylor’s injuries and the hike and climb that lay ahead. He inspected the bleeding wound the bear had left behind on Taylor’s thigh, curled his palm around her shin and squeezed. “Let’s get you cleaned up. It’s time we found a way out of here.”

Chapter Twelve

Headstones were not a good sign.

Taylor stopped in the center of a small cemetery, her sweaty skin prickling under the cool shade of thick trees towering around the overgrown space.

"This can't be right." Andi, her limp more pronounced, hobbled out of the thick tree line and bit her lip as she stared at the weathered grave site. "What's a graveyard doing in the middle of nowhere?"

"It's historic." Taylor bent, rubbed her tired eyes and inspected an aged headstone. The elements had taken their toll, leaving black tinges on the edges of the stone, and green algae had spread across its center, obscuring most of the markings. "From the late 1800s to early 1900s, probably."

Will, standing several feet ahead, surveyed the tangle of trees, shrubs and foliage obscuring the terrain that lay before them. "We're in deep backcountry. No telling what we'll stumble across." He glanced back at them, concern in his dark eyes. "Keep your eyes and ears open. Stick together and keep talking. We've got a lot more ground to cover."

And after that, they'd have to climb five thousand feet to reach the crag and hope the rescue helicopter returned at just the right time. It was a long shot at best, but there was no alternative.

Taylor rubbed her weary eyes. Three hours ago, they'd sat by the stream for a little while, washing their wounds, refilling the empty water bottles and collecting themselves after the bear attack—and her grief-stricken confession over Preston's death.

She stilled, waiting for familiar emotions to assail her at the memory—guilt, shame and condemnation. But…they didn't come.

Instead, a sensation of exhausted relief had replaced the turmoil that had clamored inside her for years, and the brief unsettled feeling she'd experienced at the sight of the headstones began to ease. It was as though confessing her actions out loud had helped lighten the heavy burden she'd carried for so long, and Will's reassurance that she could be forgiven had nourished the hope that struggled to bloom within her heart, allowing it to grow and unfurl fully in her chest. It had stayed with her during the two hours they'd hiked after leaving the campsite and made their way to the ravine, though their progress had been slowed by injury, hunger and exhaustion.

But even now, that hope resurfaced as she joined Will in examining the imposing path that lay ahead, the miles that separated them from a chance of being rescued and the ever-increasing ascent to the rocky outlook.

"We can do it," she said. Just not alone.

I believe there's nothing we could ever do or not do that would cause Him to abandon us.

"Yeah." Will smiled—tired but sincere—and looked at Andi. "How you holding up?"

Andi lifted her chin and smiled back, but it was forced. "I'm good. Let's keep going."

"Not quite yet." Taylor crossed the clearing and eyed Andi's shin. "You're bleeding again."

Bright scarlet blood had seeped through the makeshift bandage wrapped around her leg, and it had begun to trickle toward her injured ankle.

Taylor crouched beside Andi, wincing as her tight muscles screamed in protest, and carefully began peeling off the soaked cloth. "Lean on me so you don't strain your ankle and let me know if it starts to hurt too much."

Andi flinched and a cry of pain left her lips, but when Taylor paused in removing the dressing, she looked down at Taylor and motioned for her to continue.

After peeling off the blood-soaked dressing, Taylor grabbed a bottle of filtered water from the dry bag she carried and, watching Andi's face for signs of discomfort, poured it carefully over the wound, washing away bits of dirt and the trickle of blood.

"You're good at this," Andi said, placing a hand on Taylor's shoulder for balance and peering down at her injury.

Taylor paused then, satisfied the wound was clean

again, returned the water bottle to the dry bag and ripped another strip of cloth off the bottom of her shirt. "I've had a lot of practice."

A tense silence filled the space between them. Then Andi asked softly, "Because of your husband?"

Grimacing, Taylor nodded, then proceeded to wrap the strip of cloth around Andi's shin.

Andi squeezed her shoulder gently, stilling her movements. "I'm sorry. I wish that hadn't happened to you."

Taylor looked up and smiled. "Thank you."

Andi leaned closer. "I wish things had been different," she said. "For all of us."

Taylor slowly tied the fabric into a snug knot. "What kinds of things?"

Andi glanced at Will, who walked to the other side of the graveyard and ducked between a tangle of trees to study a different route through the ravine. "Did he tell you about my mom?"

"A little."

"That she left us?"

Taylor stood. "Yes."

Andi released Taylor's shoulder and looked down at her bandage. Her fingers picked at the fabric, testing the knot. "Did you know your mom when you were my age?"

"No. I never met her."

Andi looked up again, her brown eyes seeking Taylor's. "What about your dad?"

"I never knew him, either."

She was silent for a moment, then said, "My dad told

me last night that he thought you might be on your own. He said he tries to remember that everyone struggles with something, and that it's important to save room in his heart to be kind and help others when he can." Face flushing, she winced. "I'm sorry I haven't been more welcoming to you lately."

Taylor smiled gently. "It's okay. You're pretty lucky, you know? Having a dad like yours. He loves you very much."

The sadness in her expression eased as she glanced across the clearing again, one corner of her mouth lifting in a small grin when Will reemerged from the trees. "Yeah. He's pretty fantastic. Even if he does get on my nerves sometimes."

Taylor laughed. "I'm guessing that's usually what happens when dads are looking out for their daughters. I'd be worried if he didn't get on your nerves once in a while. Wouldn't you? At least that's one way you know how much he cares."

The little mouth hitch turned into a full-blown, pleased grin. "I suppose."

Will, sipping from a bottle of water, halted midstep in their direction, lowered the bottle and narrowed his eyes at Taylor. "She's not sharing more disastrous moments from our camping trips, is she?"

Nope. She's just proving even more what a wonderful dad—and man—you are.

Heart skipping, Taylor kept that pleasant thought to herself, cocked her head to the side and grinned. "How many disastrous moments were there?"

Will smirked. "More than I'd care to revisit."

"Then you better keep us moving before Andi has a chance to remember another one." Taylor motioned toward the overgrown paths behind him. "Which way do you think is the straightest shot to the outcrop?"

"Hard to tell," he said. "But my best guess would be the one on the left. There's a narrow trail that winds down the mountain a ways, and I can hear water moving farther down the path. We need to refill the water bottles again, and that might be a good place to do it."

"I'm starving," Andi said. "How much farther do you think it'll be until we make it to the outcrop?"

"Don't know. Might have a better idea when we reach the bottom of the trail." Will frowned, tipped his head back and looked at the sky. "But it's taking us longer than I planned, so we may need to regroup when we reach the stream. Decide if we want to chance tackling the outcrop today or camp one more night."

Taylor glanced up, too, noting the slow swing of the sun toward the western part of the sky. Unless the outcrop was right around the corner, the chances of them reaching the crag today were pretty slim.

"Might not be a bad thing if we don't make it today," Taylor said. "It'll be a strenuous climb, and a good night's rest will help us all, I think."

Nodding, Will lifted his chin at Andi. "How's your leg?"

Andi smiled. "Good. Taylor changed the bandage and fixed me up."

"And your ankle?" Will's brows rose. "I don't want you keeping pain a secret, okay? If you're hurting, you'll tell me, right? That way we can—"

"Stop and rest," Andi finished for him, her smile widening. "Yes, sir. I promise."

A slow grin spread across Will's face. "Immediate compliance. Now, that's a first." His brown eyes settled on Taylor. "Whatcha been teaching my kid?"

Taylor shrugged. "Nothing. As a matter of fact," she added, winking at Andi as she recalled the advice he'd given her, "I think she's learning from you."

A look of pride entered Will's expression, and he held her gaze a moment longer before ducking his head and motioning for them to follow. "We better get going. Sooner we reach the bottom of the trail, the sooner we'll get full water bottles and a breather."

Taylor watched him stroll toward a narrow dirt path, her attention clinging to the wide set of his shoulders and muscular profile beneath a splash of sunlight through the thick trees. For such a strong man, he was patient, considerate, and maybe even had a bit of a sensitive side, judging from what Andi had shared. Andi was indeed lucky to have him as her father. And any woman would be lucky to have him in her life at all.

Her cheeks warmed and, catching Andi's eyes on her, she held out her arm. "Why don't you lean on me? It'll make the walk downhill easier."

Andi hesitated, but nodded gratefully and curled her arm around the bend in Taylor's elbow. "Thanks."

They followed Will down the winding dirt path, Andi leaning on her as they stepped over knotted roots and ducked beneath low-hanging branches. The descent was steeper than she'd anticipated, and soon beads of sweat began trickling over her temples and down her cheeks.

"How much farther?" Andi asked, her breath catching, the limp more noticeable.

"We're almost to the creek," Will said, glancing back at them.

True to his word, Will lifted a thick branch out of the way, motioning for them to proceed, and once they cleared the trees, sunlight flooded a damp moss-covered bank, and the gurgling rush of water arose in the humid summer air. Due to recent rains, the water moved high and fast.

A shudder ran through Taylor at the memory of the river's strong pull, sucking her beneath the surface. "How deep do you think it is?"

"Five, six feet, maybe," Will said, joining them on the bank. "There's a clearing on the other side." He pointed to a thick log that had fallen over the deepest part of the swift creek, forming a crude but somewhat stable bridge to the other side of the bank. "Normally, I'd say that'd be a good place to cross, but all things considered..." His gaze lingered on Andi's leg and he shook his head. "Maybe we should try swimming across instead? Or maybe finding another place to cro—"

"No," Andi said quickly. "I don't want to go back in the water yet. I'm so tired, all I want to do is crash for a while. I can make it across the log."

Taylor glanced at Andi, who leaned more heavily on her arm. The young girl's expression was determined, but her lips pressed into a thin line as though she were in pain. "What about your ankle?" she asked softly. "That log isn't a flat surface, and you'll need the use of both feet to stay balanced all the way across."

Andi frowned and glanced down at her injured ankle. "If I hold on to you, I think I could stay balanced long enough to make it across."

"Might be easier in the water," Will said. "You could hold on to the log, and Taylor and I could help y—"

"Please, Dad." Her hand tightened around Taylor's arm as she stared at the water rushing past them. "I don't want to go back in the water yet. I can do it if Taylor is okay with helping me." She looked up, her eyes searching Taylor's. "What do you think?"

Taylor studied the vulnerable shadows in her eyes and the hint of hope fighting its way into her expression. She smiled, all too aware of what Andi was feeling. That pressing need to strike out and prove herself. To move on. To reach for something better.

For so many years, Taylor had felt empty—almost dead inside. But lately, especially after her confession to Will and his reassurance that God would never abandon her, she was beginning to feel more capable than she had in a long time. And during this trip, she'd begun to feel alive—truly alive—for the first time in her life.

Taylor smiled. "I think we should go for it."

Will planted his right foot on the center of the log, reached out his left arm and carefully glanced over his shoulder. "You ready?"

Andi slipped her arm around his and nodded. “Ready.”

She didn’t sound ready. Her breath had quickened, her eyes darted over the water rushing beneath their feet and her hand clamped on to his upper arm. From the bank, the creek looked deep but unintimidating. Perched on the log, however, the scene was very different. Water, flowing fast several feet below them, crashed against stones, spraying their bare legs and arms. The steady roar of the current grew louder once they stepped onto the log, and the opposite riverbank—which had seemed no more than fifteen or twenty feet away while they stood safely on the ground beside the river—now looked as though it lay two miles away.

Will leaned forward an inch or two and glanced at Taylor, who stood on the other side of Andi, their arms entwined. “Taylor? You still up for this?”

She glanced his way, her blue eyes bright and blond hair shining beneath a hint of sunlight that broke past the tall trees lining the creek. “Let’s do it.”

He stilled, savoring the sight of her excited expression. It was mesmerizing, almost—the slow change in her demeanor that had begun to gradually appear over the past couple of days. He’d first noticed it when she’d rescued him from the river after the mudslide. Instead of breaking down in tears or losing her temper with God as he had, she’d pointed out how God had helped them and encouraged him to see the brighter side of their situation. Two nights ago, a note of hope had entered her voice as they’d watched elk graze in the meadow near the lean-to they’d constructed. And last night, she'd stood for hours with him under the sparkling night sky, admiring the stars, finding common ground with his painful past and sharing her fears.

Sometimes I can't understand why He doesn't answer. Why He doesn't help us when we need Him so badly.

He'd wondered then if she'd be able to hold on to that little bit of hope he'd glimpsed in her eyes and heard in her voice two days ago. He'd wondered even more after she'd broken down with guilt and shame by the stream hours earlier. But with every step they'd taken along the mountain over the past hours, her tears had dried, her head had lifted and her eyes had looked up—not at the mountain peaks, he thought, but perhaps farther beyond. To something, or someone, even more beautiful and a thousand times more powerful.

Those rough waters are good at pushing people closer together. Closer to God, too.

Will smiled. Good ol' Jax. As much as he hated to give the man credit, he had to admit Jax had been right so far. Not only did it seem like Taylor was beginning to heal on this mountain, but his daughter was arm in arm with him, leaning on and trusting him, and it seemed Taylor might be, too.

"Take it slow at first," Taylor said, her eyes clinging to his as she adjusted her grip on Andi's arm. "One step at a time, okay?"

Will's smile grew. "You got it," he said softly.

Will refocused on the log, its surface speckled with splashes of creek water that sparkled in the sunlight, and carefully took a step forward. The wood felt slick beneath his shoe and he stiffened, maintaining a steady footing.

"All right, Andi," he said. "Like Taylor said, take it one step at a time, okay? And hold on to us as much as you need to."

A heavy breath left her parted lips and she nodded. "Okay."

She took one step and shifted her weight forward, teetering for a second on one leg.

Will steadied her with one hand. "It's not too late to change your mind. We can always turn back and—"

"No." She dragged in a steady breath and offered a tight smile. "Thank you, but I can do it. We're all tired, and this is the fastest way across."

Pride rushed through him, quiet and comforting. It'd been a long time since Andi had set her pain aside and thought of others besides herself. This was the confident, caring young woman he'd always known she was at heart.

She nudged him, the tension in her grip easing slightly as she laughed. "Come on, Dad. You're holding up the train."

He chuckled. "Yes, ma'am."

Will stepped forward again and Andi followed slowly, squeezing his arm tight as she shifted her weight and regained her balance. Taylor waited until Andi was steady on the log, and she'd follow, moving slowly along the log and supporting Andi with her hand on her elbow.

They continued across the log, one small step after another, the swift creek below them roaring loudly when they reached the center of the log, drowning out

Will's voice as he guided Andi and Taylor's praise as she complimented Andi on her progress.

By the time they reached the last quarter of the log, the sun had dipped farther in the sky, Andi had stumbled twice and her arm shook in Will's hold.

"We're almost there, baby," he said, eyeing the length of the log, then the bank. "Three feet, maybe four, and we're there."

She nodded jerkily, refocused on the log and took another step. Her foot slipped across the wet bark and her arms flailed wildly in his and Taylor's grip.

Andi squealed, rocking back and forth within their hold. Will firmed his grip on her, bent his knees and squatted down a few inches to regain his balance. Taylor followed suit, and moments later, the swaying stopped and they stood as one again, steady and balanced, cold creek water spraying their faces and necks.

Taylor's soft laughter rang out above the water. "And to think, you almost backed out of this trip, Will."

Panic receded from Andi's face and she smiled. "Good thing I talked him back into it."

Lips quirking, Will cocked an eyebrow. "Y'all wanna hold on to that thought until after we reach the bank? We still have a couple feet left to go."

Grins still plastered on their faces, they nodded.

Hiding his own smile, Will resumed the slow pace toward the bank and they followed, eventually making it safely to dry ground.

Andi sagged against him in exhausted relief. "Thank goodness that's over."

Will bent low, scooped her up in his arms and

hefted her snug against his chest. “Let’s get you somewhere where you can rest for a while.” Glancing over his shoulder, he called back to Taylor as he walked, “There’s a soft patch of grass on the other side of the clearing. I’m gonna get Andi settled and get a fire started. It’s too late to tackle the last stretch to the overlook, so we’ll camp here for the night and head out first thing in the morning.”

Taylor shifted the dry bag she carried off her shoulders, lowered it on the ground and began rummaging inside. “I’ll fill the water bottles at the creek, then join you.”

Thanking her, Will strolled across the clearing, squinting against the glare of the late-afternoon sun as it slowly lowered behind the treetops. The sporadic chatter of birds began to slow, a rhythmic chorus of crickets began and a cooler breeze drifted over the creek and across the clearing.

Squatting, Will gently eased Andi to the ground, removed her shoes and checked her injuries. Her ankle was puffy—which was to be expected after such a long hike—but the bandage on her leg was in great shape and would last through the night without needing to be changed.

“Taylor did a good job fixing you up,” he said, sitting on the grass beside Andi.

“Yeah.” She wiped sweat from her eyes and peered down at her bandaged wound, a sad note entering her tone. “She said she’s had a lot of practice.”

Anger sparked in Will’s gut and he curled his fingers into the thick grass, forming fists. His eyes sought

Taylor's graceful form as she walked near the creek, crouching down and filling one water bottle, and then another. After filling the last bottle, she sat down on the bank, and when a crow flapped its big wings overhead, she looked up and smiled as it soared past.

He frowned, his chest aching at the thought of another man putting his hands on her. Hurting her. How could Preston have done it? How could he have married her, professed to love her and harmed her in such a way?

That kind of anger and violence he'd never understand. And Taylor deserved so much better. She deserved a man who appreciated her sharp mind and generous heart. Who respected her thoughts and beliefs. Who'd protect her and cherish her. A man like…

"You like her a lot, don't you?"

Andi was staring at him now, her narrowed eyes traveling slowly over his face.

"Yeah," he said softly, meeting her direct gaze head-on. "I do."

Andi studied him a moment longer, then turned away, her attention settling on Taylor in the distance. "I know I said that I wanted it to just be you and me." She picked at the grass, her fingers trailing through the long blades. "But some of today was kinda nice, you know?" She frowned. "Not the bear or Taylor being sad and all, but after. When she helped me on the hike. And when you were both helping me get across the creek. That was kinda nice." She glanced at Taylor again. "Working together like that, it was kind of like being a…"

"Team?" Will bit his lip, studying the play of emotions across Andi's face.

"Maybe. But it felt like more than that. It felt like…"

"Family?"

Andi looked at him then, her eyes meeting his, the same longing that throbbed in his chest reflected in her sad smile. "Yeah," she said, her voice hesitant. Surprised. "It felt like family."

Chapter Thirteen

Sunlight coaxed Will from a deep sleep. He blinked slowly against a thin ray of golden light that strolled across the grassy clearing, traveled over his feet and legs, then up his chest to settle over his cheek.

Inhaling, he stretched his arms overhead and flexed his legs, loosening his sore biceps and calves. His fingers bumped something soft and he rolled his head to the side to find Andi curled into a ball, sleeping deeply, beside him. Taylor, her cheek resting on her hand as she lay on the other side of Andi, still slept, too.

Smiling, Will refocused on the sky above them. The day was just getting started, the sun having only just begun peeking above the mountain peaks, and a burst of color painted the sky in hues of gold, pink and purple. A light mist hovered over the clearing, leaving his skin cool and relaxed, and he fought to keep his eyes open, the exhausting events of the past several days threatening to drag him back to sleep despite the lofty goal they'd planned for today.

Hours earlier, after Taylor had refilled the water bottles at the creek and rejoined him and Andi in the clearing, he'd built a fire and they all three had scavenged some nuts and berries in the bushes along the tree line, taking great care to stick together and keep an eye out for bears. Thankfully, the excursion had been uneventful, and by nightfall, the fire was flickering brightly beneath the stars. Bellies full and eyes heavy, they'd stayed up a while longer, lounging in the soft grass and pointing out constellations in the heavens. Andi had drifted off first and Taylor second, leaving him alone with his thoughts for another hour until he'd finally succumbed to sleep, as well.

Strangely enough, last night had been one of the most peaceful rests he'd ever had. A velvet sky full of stars, Andi's deep, peaceful breathing as she slept—the sound just as comforting now as it had been years ago when he'd checked on her in her crib at night—and the knowledge that Taylor was nearby, a part of their journey, had set his mind at ease. His prayers for a safe hike to the outcrop today had come easy, and sleep had sneaked up on him even more easily.

So much so, he didn't want to move at all from his grassy bed, despite the fact that they needed every drop of daylight they could capture for the journey to the outcrop.

His eyes fluttered closed and he'd almost drifted into a light sleep again when a soft drumlike beat whispered in the distance. The beating of wings. A hawk, maybe? Or a crow? It was too early to be an ow—

Will bolted upright, the earth tilting for a moment

until his eyes focused on the misty clearing, swift-moving creek, then the mountain range that rose before him. He tilted his head, listening intently.

The sound receded, then renewed again, the steady rhythmic whirl very faint but discernible.

"Chopper." He shot to his feet, shook Andi awake first, then Taylor. "Up! Get up. We've got to get going."

He grabbed the water bottles that were scattered on the ground near the blackened remains of the fire and shoved them in the dry bag.

"What's wrong?" Andi, sitting up, rubbed her eyes.

"The helicopter's out." He stilled, motioning toward the mountain range in the distance as Taylor sat up and pushed her blond hair out of her face. "You hear that?"

Taylor tilted her head and eyed the sky. "Yeah. But it sounds like it's going in the other direction."

"Probably." He bent over the dry bag and secured it closed. "That's why we need to get going."

Taylor frowned and shook her head, a sleepy expression on her face. "So we're changing the plan? We're going to follow the helicopter instead?"

"Nope." Will stood and slung the dry bag over his shoulders. "We're going to the outcrop and we're going to climb to the crag."

Andi pointed toward the mountains. "But the helicopter's going that way." She swiveled around and pointed behind her. "And you said the outcrop's in that direction, right?"

"Yep." He nudged the charred wood of the previous night's fire with his shoe to make sure it had completely burned out. "If the rescue chopper's flying a full route today, it should pass back over this area in a little while. When it does, we need to be at the top of that outcrop, visible and ready to signal for help."

"How do you know it'll come back?" Andi asked, peering up at him.

He hesitated, glancing over his shoulder at the empty—and now silent—sky. "I don't. Not for sure."

Eyes lowering, she bit her lip. "What if we hike all that way and it doesn't show up?"

"It might happen, but I don't think it will," he said through stiff lips, hoping the uncertainty moving through him didn't emerge in his voice. "This is our best shot at getting help. We need to..." He spread his hands, searching for words. Searching for strength he wasn't sure he had left to ensure they made it safely out of the ravine and up another mountain for a rescue that may or may not come through for them. "We just have to..."

"Have faith." Taylor stood. "We have to have faith that it'll return. It almost found us once. We just have to believe that, this time, it'll show up again and get us out of here. That when we get to the top of that crag, we won't be alone." She met his eyes and smiled, the warm look of gratitude in hers lifting his spirits. "We'll keep talking to God and have faith that He'll answer."

Will nodded, admiring the hopeful light in her eyes and determined expression despite the dark circles of exhaustion under her eyes. "Yeah," he whispered. "He'll answer."

"Okay," Andi said, standing slowly. She winced as her injured ankle took her weight. "Let's go to the outcrop."

Will's heart sank as he eyed her ankle. Purple and red bruising had spread across the pale swollen flesh, wrapping around her ankle and marring her puffy heel. He knelt beside her, cupped her calf in his palm and gently lifted her foot, inspecting it closely.

It didn't look good. As a matter of fact, it—

"I'm fine." Andi's hand squeezed his shoulder. "I can make it to the outcrop."

He glanced up, a sweet mix of pride and admiration running through him at the determined tilt of her chin and confident set of her shoulders. "It's obvious you're in pain, Andi. And it's a long hike from here to the outcrop."

"I promise, I won't slow you down."

"I'm not worried about that," he said, easing her foot back to the ground. "I'm worried about you injuring yourself even more." Sighing, he eased back on his haunches and studied the rugged landscape in the distance. A sense of urgency spiked through him as he glanced at the still silent sky. "I'm familiar with these mountains and have a better shot at getting there faster." He glanced at Taylor. "If Taylor agrees, you and she could stay here and I'll hik—"

"No." Andi shook her head, her long brown hair spilling over her shoulders. "I don't want to split up again. What if something were to happen to you? What if—?"

"I'll be fine."

"But I won't know that for sure." Her voice broke and moisture glistened along her lashes. "I don't want to separate again. I won't know where you are, if you're okay or if I'll ever see you again." She shook her head. "I'd rather my ankle hurt during the hike than to sit here wondering whether you're okay or not."

Will rose and cupped her face in his hands, sweeping his thumbs gently across her cheeks. "Okay. We'll go together." He glanced at her shoes. "Let's see if we can get your shoes on. You're not hiking barefoot."

It took several minutes to get Andi's shoe on her injured foot. The swelling from her ankle injury had traveled down to her heel and toes, and after loosening the shoelaces and gingerly testing different angles, Will and Taylor finally managed to get the shoe in place and laced tightly enough that it was secure. Then they looped one of Andi's arms through one of their own and, positioned on either side of her, they helped her take her first slow steps of the morning across the clearing to loosen her tender muscles.

When they made it to the tree line, Andi's pace picked up and Taylor smiled. "There. I think we've gotten a steady rhythm. Just don't go running off on us."

A weak laugh burst from Andi in between heavy breaths. "There's absolutely no chance of that."

The first mile through thick woods and thorny brush was hard, but when they emerged from the ravine and reached the base of the mountain Will had spoken of, the imposing trail winding up the rugged mountain to the exposed outcrop seemed grueling…and almost impossible to surmount.

During the initial hike, Andi had leaned more heavily against Will, but now she practically sagged on his arm. He eyed the increased swelling of her ankle and the stubborn jut of her jaw. Her face was beet red and sweat soaked her shirt, but she stared up at the outcrop, an eager light in her eyes as she tilted her head to the side.

"I don't hear anything," she said. "How long do you think it'll take them to come back around this way?"

Will surveyed the blue sky. The sun had risen high above the mountain range as they'd hiked from the clearing to the outcrop, warming the air to a humid heat. There wasn't a cloud in sight…or any signs of a helicopter. Only the whistle of the breeze as it swept over mountain peaks punctuated the stillness surrounding them.

"I don't know." Will hefted the dry bag more securely on his right shoulder. "But at least we're in a clearer space. Hopefully, it'll swing by on our way up and catch sight of us."

Though he had to admit, he was beginning to have his doubts. The longer the day wore on, the less chance there was of the pilot returning.

"Let's keep going," Taylor said firmly, stepping onto a crude dirt path that led toward the outcrop. "The sooner we get there, the sooner we can rest."

The encouraging note in her voice spurred them on and they hiked another mile up the snakelike trail of dirt that wound around the mountain, higher and higher into direct rays of the hot summer sun, Andi's steps slowing more and more with each step.

A hawk circled overhead, its sharp cry ringing across the mountain range. Just below it, jutting out from around the bend in the trail, was the outcrop, its bald face rising up almost like an arrow pointing at the sky, each rugged ridge leading to the summit more perilous than the one before.

Andi looked up, sweat streaming down her blazing red face, her chest heaving on ragged breaths. "Are we…almost…there?"

"You are," Will said firmly. Halting midstep, he tugged Andi to a stop, too, then led her a few steps to the left and helped her lower to a seated position, her back resting against a smooth stretch of rock wall. "There's no way you're climbing that outcrop. You need to rest."

"But I—"

"No arguments." Will shrugged the dry bag off his shoulder and withdrew a bottle of filtered water. "Here." He unscrewed the cap and pressed the bottle to her lips, holding it steady as she drank from it slowly between heavy breaths. "You stay here, keep sipping that and rest."

He moved to stand and she reached out with a shaky hand, halting him. "Stay…stay here with me."

Heart breaking at the sound of fear in her voice, Will squatted down beside her and tucked a wet strand of hair behind her ear. "I've got to climb the outcrop, Andi. The best chance we have of being spotted is on that crag."

"Then let me go." Taylor eased down beside them, glancing from him to Andi. "I can make the climb, and you can both stay here."

Will shook his head. "It's a steep climb, Taylor. Shorter than the wall we scaled by the river, but it's more dangerous. There aren't as many big holds and you'll have to pivot more than—"

"Are you saying I can't do it?"

He paused, the slight twitch of her lips dragging a laugh from deep within his worry-laden chest. "No, I know better than that. And even if I didn't, I'd know the repercussions would be enough to keep me silent on it." His smile slipped and he leaned closer to her, saying softly, "I'm just worried, is all. You've got to be as exhausted as we are and you'll be climbing blind."

"So would you, if you went. At least this way you can stay with Andi." She reached out and squeezed Andi's shoulder. "Don't worry. I'll get us some help, and no matter what happens, your dad won't leave you."

Andi lowered the water bottle with a shaky hand, her expression crumpling and tears spilling over her lashes. "You'll be careful, won't you?" Her chin quivered. "You'll come back to us?"

"Of course." Taylor leaned over, wrapped her arms around Andi and hugged her tight, smoothing a hand over her hair. "As soon as the helicopter comes back or when the sun starts to set—whichever comes first—I'll climb back down and stay with you both."

A sob shook Andi's shoulders. Will's heart warmed as Andi hugged Taylor back.

"Be careful," Andi said brokenly.

"I promise," Taylor whispered before releasing her and standing.

Will stood and walked with her, saying over his shoulder, "Stay put, Andi. I'll be back in a sec."

They rounded the corner and stood at the base of the outcrop, staring up at the steep trail of rock.

"Trust." Will cleared his throat, struggling to steady the tremor in his voice. "Free-climbing isn't about—"

"Physical strength," Taylor finished for him, facing him. "I know. A lot of what's needed," she continued softly, placing her hand gently on his chest, her warm touch settling directly over his heart, "is here."

Emotion rolled through his chest, strong and pleasant, making his breath catch. He covered her hand with his own and squeezed. "Please be careful. Take your time."

She nodded, her blue eyes lowering to his lips. "I will."

He dipped his head, pressed his forehead to hers and closed his eyes, savoring the feel of her presence. She pressed closer, her chin lifting and lips brushing his. He covered her mouth with his own, kissing her back softly, trying his best to transfer every bit of strength he had left to her, praying for her safe return.

A soft sigh of pleasure left her and he raised his head, his eyes searching the dark blue depths of hers. "You're not alone. I'll be right here if you need me."

Nodding, she slid her hand from his chest and stepped back, then walked to the base of the outcrop, felt for a secure hold and hoisted herself onto the lowest ledge.

Will's throat tightened as he watched her sweat-slicked arms and legs lift her weight higher and higher, her muscles flexing as the wind whistled past the sharp edges of the crag above.

"You know how precious she's become to me," he whispered on a quiet prayer to the silent sky above. "Move the mountain for her. Please get her there safely."

Taylor curled her fingers around the sharp edge of stone, wincing as it cut the tender flesh of her palm. She looked over her shoulder at the drop below, a sense of dread snaking through her at the sight of hard rocks and thorny brush. But that was nothing compared to the summit of the outcrop. The crag was little more than a narrow wedge jutting out from the mountain itself, planted atop the mountain she, Andi and Will had climbed, almost five thousand feet above the ground.

Look up.

The deep tones of Will's voice whispered through her mind and she faced the huge stone in front of her and inhaled slowly.

"Keep looking up," she reminded herself. "That's where I'm headed."

Or at least that was where she'd been heading for the past half hour. Only, with each foot she climbed, she left Andi and Will farther behind, and soon they were out of sight, and she was on her own.

She rested briefly, perched there on the side of the outcrop, her hands holding the ledge above her and her toes planted on the ledge below, and rolled her lips, recalling Will's kiss. The feel of his tender kiss still lingered on her lips, warming her skin and sending a rush of strength through her chest, lifting her spirit.

You're not alone.

She looked up again and focused on a small wisp of a cloud in the distance, its white contours flexing with the wind's current, stretching and shifting along with the breeze across the sky. A heavier gust of wind swept over the mountain. Then silence settled, her raspy breaths the only sound on the ledge.

Arms trembling, she pressed closer to the rock's face. She wasn't alone—she'd truly begun to believe that. If only He'd speak or send a sign…anything so long as it offered reassurance and gave her the strength she needed to ascend the remaining feet of imposing stone.

Sweat stung her eyes and she blinked hard, wincing as her eyes burned. Thoughts muddled in her mind, tangling together in phrases and half-formed sentences, the toll of the past few days sinking past her skin, through her muscles, and seeping into her bones, making her body feel heavy and sluggish.

Fatigue and soreness washed over her. Her thighs shook and a cramp knotted in the sole of her right foot, forcing her to curl tighter to the rocky face to which she clung, and she bit back a pained cry.

"What did your pops used to say, Jax?" She forced herself to speak, to ask the question out loud and regain her focus. "On the bank, what did you mention he used to say?"

Her disjointed thoughts, whirling together, began to part, easing away from each other, and one memory solidified in her weary mind.

When the world broke a man, all he had to do was come to God's land and let Him know he's here.

"That's all I need to do, right?" she asked, grabbing the thought and holding on to it. Centering it in her mind. "I just have to let You know I'm here."

Sucking in a strong breath, she tightened her grip on the ledge above, pulled hard and hoisted her body onto the next landing.

"It's taken me a long time to get this far." Voice trembling, she continued praying. "And I'm hoping You'll help me along a little bit further."

The next good hold was to the right, at least three feet away, and she'd have to shift her weight to one leg to reach it.

"I'm asking for another chance," she prayed softly. "A chance to get my feet under me and start over."

She lifted her right leg, shifting her weight to the side, and balancing on her left foot, she focused on the ledge up ahead, homing in on the most secure place to grab.

"Please forgive me for not trusting You. Please help me find a way forward."

Inhaling, she held her breath and lunged upward, her hand landing in the right spot—the perfect place she'd homed in on—and her right foot settled on a small, safe rock two feet above her. She immediately dragged her left leg up, balanced on both feet and regained her bearings.

A swift breeze swept over the outcrop, cooling her overheated skin, and she tipped her chin up, breathing deeply. Just feet above her, the crag jutted out over her head, a smooth bare shelf of rock that offered an unimpeded view of the mountain range and skyline.

But the next move would be tricky. There was only one choice to make—a straight upward lunge toward the shelf, quick grab and pull…or a longer, unpredictable route around the crag with the hope that the path, unviewable from this angle, would be clear enough to scale to the summit.

A cut on her palm began to bleed, coating her skin with blood, causing her hold to slip. She scrambled with her left hand, pulling harder and leaning to the left, her obliques screaming at the abrupt movement.

"I'm here…" she whispered, her legs aching. "Please help me. Which way do I go?"

Her grip slipped again, her right hand losing its hold, and she flailed briefly, the tips of her toes straining to maintain their balance on the lower jut of rock and her left hand clamping down on the rough rock beneath her fingertips.

"Please—" Her voice broke, a sense of dread sinking her spirit, weighing her down even further. "Which way?"

A soft throbbing sound echoed in the distance. The rapid beat mingled with the pounding of her heart, drawing closer and growing louder. Faint cries peppered the air, the sharp calls barely discernible, but the sound drifted up the mountain, reaching her ears, speeding up her heart.

The helicopter!

She rolled her head carefully to the left and there it was, just a small dark speck in the blue sky, but headed in the direction of the outcrop. Glancing over her shoulder, she hoped to catch a glimpse of Andi or Will, but saw nothing but jagged ledges and a spine-snapping drop to the ground below.

The shouts returned, so very faint and far away that they barely carried on the breeze, but she heard them all the same. Heard Andi and Will urging her on, even though she couldn't see them.

Adrenaline spiking, she dragged her wet hand over her soggy shorts, managed to wipe most of the blood away, then eyed the thrust of the crag above her.

"I'm here," she shouted, the sound hoarse. Weak.

The whip of helicopter blades drew closer, whirling louder, faster.

Lunging upward, Taylor grabbed the crag with her right hand, then left, and yanked, hauling herself up and over the sharply angled ledge, her legs dangling precariously in the air for a few moments as she dragged her lower body onto the smooth landing.

"I'm here!" Muscles seizing and body throbbing with pain, she shoved to her feet, lifted her arms high above her head and waved. "Over here! We're over here!"

The dark speck drew nearer and nearer, increasing in size, the distinctive shape of the helicopter sharpening as it approached.

Hot tears streaming down her cheeks, Taylor reached higher and waved her arms faster, hope flooding her heart as the helicopter flew over her, then circled back, slowing as it headed toward the crag, then hovered above her.

Dropping her head back, she smiled heavenward, the rhythmic throb of the helicopter's blades pounding in time with the beat of her heart as hope flooded her soul and filled her eyes with a fresh surge of happy tears.

God hadn't abandoned her. He was right here with her, had been all along—even during her darkest times—residing within her heart and leading her to a safer place and better life. He'd led her here, to safety and strength. To Will and Andi.

Chapter Fourteen

"Do you know where you want to go?"

Taylor swallowed a hefty swig of cherry-flavored soda, savored the sweet fizz of carbonated water on her dry tongue and opened her eyes.

A nurse stood in front of her, writing notes on a clipboard. He stopped writing, tucked the pen behind his left ear and smiled. "Slight dehydration, minor lacerations and no broken bones. You were lucky, all things considered." He crossed his arms, the clipboard tucked against his chest. "Dr. Hamilton's cleared you, so you're free to go. I can buzz the front desk if you want? They'd be happy to call a cab for you and you could be on your way in less than ten minutes to wherever it is you'd like to go."

Taylor stared at him for a moment, absorbing his words, letting the moment sink in. For the first time in her life, she'd spent no more than half an hour in a doctor's presence and been cleared to leave in less than that amount of time with a smile and well wishes.

No one had questioned her endlessly about the cuts on her leg and hands. There'd been no skeptical glances or intense stares full of pity. Just a quick examination and wound cleaning, brief surprise and sympathy for the disastrous rafting trip she'd endured and the cold can of cherry-flavored soda she'd requested from the hospital cafeteria's vending machine pressed into her bandaged palm.

All in all, it was the best experience she'd ever had in a hospital. And not once had her skin clammed up or her hands shaken while sitting on the narrow hospital bed in close confines with the male doctor and nurse.

"…anything else?"

Taylor blinked and shook her head, refocusing on the nurse. "I'm sorry. What did you say?"

"I asked if you had any questions or needed anything else before we get you checked out."

She tipped the can up, drained the last bit of soda and grinned. "Could I have one more of these, please? Or will I be overcharged and sent a horrendous bill later?"

He grinned back. "Oh, you've done this before, huh?"

"Yeah." She tensed, but the memories that briefly moved through her mind were not nearly as painful as they had been in the past, and her smile remained.

"Don't worry. There's a gentleman waiting for you in the lobby. He's footing the bill." The nurse turned and headed for the door, saying over his shoulder as he left, "Take your time. The soda and your friend will be waiting for you when you're ready."

Her heart skipped. *Will.*

After the nurse left, Taylor grabbed her shoes by the chair, put them on, left the hospital room and made her way down the hall to the lobby. It wasn't very busy; the late-afternoon crowd that filled the waiting room had thinned out since she, Andi and Will had arrived in the emergency room several hours ago.

It'd taken a little while to load everyone into the rescue helicopter, and the flight to the nearest hospital had lasted around forty-five minutes. When they'd arrived, Andi had been taken back immediately and Will had gone with her. Taylor had been taken to a different room later, and she had yet to hear how either of them were doing. But maybe Will was waiting for her right now.

Taylor scanned the waiting room, skimming over at least a dozen empty chairs and several strangers before her gaze settled on a familiar face.

"There you are," Jax said, standing. He held a can of cherry-flavored soda in one hand and a hesitant smile creased his cheeks. "I was just about to go back there and rustle up a doctor with some answers." His good humor dimmed as he took in her appearance, and he grimaced. "Well, that's if you wanted me to. Wouldn't blame you if you didn't want to see or talk to me."

She studied his face, long gray beard and embarrassed expression, and bit back a smile, so grateful he was still in one piece, alive, healthy and standing tall.

"Can't say I've ever let a rafting customer down so badly before." He picked at his jeans, rubbed his flushed forehead. "I won't blame you if you kick me in the shin. You can kick me in both shins if you want. It was my fault y'all got stuck out there with no—"

Laughter burst from her lips. She walked across the room, threw her arms around him and squeezed. "It's so good to see you, Jax."

He rocked back on his heels for a moment, then slung his arms around her and hugged her back. "Well, now..." He choked up a bit. "This is a surprise, but I'll take it."

She laughed once more, then released him and stepped back, drinking in the safe and sound sight of him. "I'm glad you made it out of the river safely. What about Be—?"

"Beth and Martin are fine. Just fine." He dragged in a deep breath and shook his head slightly. "Though I still have no idea how we managed to crawl out from under that raft and out of those rapids."

"I bet you were praying."

Jax stilled and studied her face. "Yeah." He nodded slowly. "Yeah, I was."

Taylor grinned. "That'll do the trick. A little prayer goes a long way. It's something I learned on your rafting trip."

He raised an eyebrow. "Did you now?"

"Yep. Among a whole host of other things."

Jax watched her closely a moment more, then held out the can of soda and smiled. "I believe you ordered this?"

"I did." She accepted it, popped the top and took a long sip, then sighed with gratitude. "Thank you so much. You have no idea how good this tastes after days of drinking filtered river water."

He gave a knowing smirk. "Oh, yeah, I do. Had to make do with it myself for a while a few years ago when I was stuck in a similar predicament." He held up a finger, retrieved something from his chair and held it out. "I believe this belongs to you."

"My camera." Taylor picked it up, her fingers seeking out familiar placements as she tilted it to and fro, checking for damage. She turned it on and immediately a photo of the river appeared in the digital frame. More pictures popped up as she scrolled through, the last photos she'd taken from the banks of Bear's Tooth River, the rapids crashing below. "Amazing," she said softly. "Nothing looks cracked or broken, and everything seems exactly as it should be."

"Yep. You packed it well in a dry bag and we found it floating a couple miles downriver the first day we went searching for y'all. Just a shame you didn't have it with you while you were stranded out there. If nothing else, I bet you came across some fantastic sights." A serious note entered his voice. "By the way, did you find what you were looking for out there?"

"Indeed," she said, laughing. "As a matter of fact, I got a very close-up view of the falls the first day when I plunged over them." Taylor smiled wider, her heart filling with so much hope it spilled over, sending a peaceful sensation through her. "And I found something else I didn't even know I was looking for."

"Well." Jax shrugged. "Maybe next time you take

a trip, you'll be able to snap a few pics of an even better view. Got any ideas where you want to go next?"

Yeah. She sure did. And the photos she imagined in her mind weren't of waterfalls or rivers, but of two people who'd become very important to her.

She shook her head. "Doesn't matter where I go next." The more important consideration was with whom. "Things turned out well on this trip, though," she continued. "Better than well, actually, considering what happened. How'd you, Beth and Martin make it off the mountain?"

"Chopper," he said, smiling. "Found us hiking up the riverbank the second day. And believe me, it wasn't a moment too soon. Beth enjoyed the raft well enough, but she sure ain't no happy camper when it comes to the kind of camping we were forced to do. First thing Beth did when we made it back to dry land was rent a hotel suite with a Jacuzzi. Don't think she's left that room yet. But that's understandable, considering it rained on us for hours that first night before we managed to find a bit of shelter."

"Same thing happened to us. Will and I spent the first night in a cave..." Her voice trailed off as she glanced around the lobby again, searching for the sight of him. "Where is Will, by the way? And Andi? Do you know if she's okay?"

Jax nodded and held up a comforting hand. "Yeah. She's all right. Came out with a banged-up ankle—which I suspect you already know. They had to stitch up a cut on her leg, and she's dehydrated, so they hooked her up to some fluids. Gonna keep her for at least one night to make sure she's good to go."

Taylor hesitated. "And Will?"

Jax tilted his head and studied her expression, a slow smile appearing. "He's with Andi. Doing fine, by all accounts." He gestured toward double doors on the other side of the room. "They're in a room down that hall. I only got back there once to check on them. Then the doc shooed me out to sew up Andi's stitches. Said no more visitors except family."

She bit her lip as a nurse opened the double doors and exited the hall, peering between the gap in the doors for a better view of the hallway. "I'd just like to see them. Make sure they're both okay. Do you think they'd let me in for a sec?"

Jax grinned, a mischievous look sparking in his eyes. "Oh, I think I can find a way to get you in."

Will shoved his hands in his pockets and stared out the small hospital room window. Night had fallen and stars sparkled brightly in the sky above the parking lot outside. He ducked his head a bit and grinned, his cheeks warming at the remembered feel of Taylor's hand inside his own, her palm pressing tight to his.

And even more comforting was the memory of Taylor sticking close by Andi's side as they'd traveled in the helicopter to the hospital. Despite her own lingering pain and exhaustion from the past few days, she'd put Andi's needs before her own, holding her hand during the flight, speaking softly when Andi had become nervous and walking by Andi's side from the helicopter into the hospital up until the moment the nurse helped Andi into a wheelchair and wheeled her down the hall.

When Andi had been wheeled into a room, helped into a bed and examined by a doctor, his focus had turned solely to Andi's well-being. He'd watched as her injuries were tended to and listened carefully to directions as to how to care for the wounds and replace the bandage on her leg. He'd been overjoyed when Jax had joined them, safe and sound, and stifled his laughter as Jax had grumbled when the doctor urged him out of the room. Then he'd sat by Andi's bedside for over an hour, smoothing a hand over her hair like he'd used to do when she was a little girl, until she'd fallen asleep. Once assured she'd drifted off into a peaceful sleep, he'd eased to the window to stretch his legs.

Now his thoughts returned to Taylor, and he longed to slip out of the room and seek her out. Verify for himself that she was safe and well.

But he wouldn't leave Andi. Not when there was a chance she'd wake up without him here. Not to mention…there was this nagging feeling in the back of his mind. This unsettling concern that maybe the feelings he'd begun to hope Taylor had for him may have been a result of circumstance. A fluke, even. Just one of those things that happened under extreme stress or unusual circumstances.

Maybe here, back in his small hometown of Stone Creek, Taylor wouldn't feel the same. The rural community was probably a great deal different than the places she'd lived and toured as a travel photographer. And who knew how long she'd stay?

His gut hollowed, an uneasy sensation flowing through him. For all he knew, she may have already left Stone Creek. She might've checked out of the hospital, caught a cab and traveled straight to the airport.

No. He shook his head. That was something Heather would've done, not Taylor. But even so…what if she didn't feel the same way about him? What if the intense emotions she stirred within him were one-sided? It'd been so long since he'd dated, let alone fallen in love, that he—

The door creaked open. He turned around to find Taylor peeking around the door.

"I'm sorry," she whispered, glancing at Andi's sleeping form. "I didn't mean to wake her or intrude." She started backing away. "I'll just slip out and—"

"No," he whispered back. His heart beat faster as he crossed the room and eased the door open a bit more. "Please come in."

She hesitated for a moment, then slipped into the room and stepped back as he shut the door behind her.

"How'd you get past the stone-cold guard?" he teased.

Taylor grinned. "I've got connections." Concern darkened her eyes. "Do you mind? I don't want to disturb Andi or—"

"No, not at all. I'm happy you came." He kneaded the back of his neck, weighing his words. "Matter of fact, I was just thinking of you."

A blush bloomed along her cheekbones. "You were?"

He nodded. "How'd your doctor visit go? Everything okay?"

"Yeah. It was short and sweet. Best hospital visit

I've ever had. It was a breeze compared to..." The blush in her cheeks darkened to a deep scarlet and she looked away, her gaze settling on Andi. "How's she doing?"

"Good." Will glanced at Andi, who still slept peacefully, hoping to distract himself from the raw emotions that surged within him at the mention of the abuse Taylor had endured from her ex-husband. "She's doing really well. A few stitches today, and she'll be checked again tomorrow morning. If she's rehydrated and still doing well, they say they'll release her to come home."

"That's great news." Taylor placed a can of cherry soda gently on the table beside Andi's bed, then lifted another can toward him. "I brought you both something. Well, Jax did, actually. He's provided me with a steady supply of soda, so I thought I'd share."

Will smiled as he took the soda. "You saw Jax?" At her nod, he added, "He was worried about you and felt awful for what happened. I told him it wasn't his fault but—"

"I told him the same thing, so maybe it'll finally sink in." She held his gaze, her blue eyes clinging to his. "Actually, I thanked him."

"For the trip?"

"Yeah," she said softly. "If it hadn't been for his ad highlighting the falls, I'd have never joined this trip or met you and Andi."

He waited, searching her expression, then studied her soft smile. Pleasure stirred in his chest as he remembered the kiss they'd shared on the outcrop, a surge of tenderness moving through him along with the desire to protect and comfort.

"I'm glad we met, too." He lifted his hand, sifted his fingers through the soft fall of her hair and trailed his fingertips across the freckles scattered along her cheek. "And I was hoping you'd feel the same after all we've been through."

She leaned into his touch, curling her hand around his and closing her eyes briefly, then rose on her toes and brushed her lips across his stubbled cheek. "Thank you."

He forced his eyes open—they had drifted shut at the soft touch of her mouth—and tried to focus on her words. "For what?"

"For saving my life," she whispered.

He brought her hand to his lips, kissed her wrist gently and smiled. "We saved each other."

Sheets rustled across the room and he lowered their clasped hands and slowly released her, then strolled across the room to Andi's bedside.

Her eyes fluttered open and she focused on him, a sleepy smile appearing. "Hey, Dad."

"Hey." He smoothed her hair back from her forehead. "How you feeling?"

Andi tilted her head back slightly and stretched her legs a little, flinching when her injured leg flexed. "Sore, but okay otherwise." She rolled her head gingerly to the side and eyed the IV that delivered fluids through her arm, glanced down at her legs and then noticed Taylor standing across the room. "Taylor." Her eyes widened a bit. "You came."

Taylor nodded and crossed to the other side of the bed. "Of course. I told you I would, and besides, I wanted to make sure for myself that you were doing okay."

Andi gestured toward the sheet, frustration briefly crossing her expression. "If it wasn't for my ankle and stitches, I'd probably walk on out of here tonight."

Taylor smiled. "Let's not rush it, okay? We're just glad you're doing better, and one night in the hospital won't hurt as long as they're taking good care of you, which I can see they are." She motioned toward the overstuffed chair by the bed. "May I?"

Andi nodded.

Taylor sat, then grabbed the soda from the table and held it up. "Feel like a taste of cherry soda?"

Laughing when Andi nodded eagerly, she popped the top, lifted the can to Andi's lips and waited patiently as Andi lifted her head and took a sip.

Andi licked her lips and issued a sound of pleasure. "Mmm. That tastes wonderful." A heavy sigh escaped her. "If only I had a double cheeseburger to go with it."

Will chuckled. "I'll run down to the cafeteria in a minute and see if they're still serving. If not, I'll ask Jax to pick us up a bag of burgers from one of the fast-food joints around the corner." His stomach growled at the thought of food and he rubbed it. "Way I feel right now, I could eat about three of 'em."

"Taylor?" Andi fiddled with the hem of her sheet, then asked, "Will you stay?"

Will's breath caught at the vulnerable note in Andi's voice and he moved closer, placing his hand on hers.

"Do you…?" Taylor glanced up at him, concern

flashing in her eyes. "Do you mean here in the hospital tonight?"

She nodded, then added, "And maybe in Stone Creek? Just for a while?"

Will tensed. "Andi, I don't thi—"

"There's a lot more to do here than people think," she rushed out. "There are lots of rapids and hiking trails. And there's a big park downtown. If you catch it just right, you can see three dozen lightning bugs in one place. It's pretty amazing."

Taylor hesitated. "Well, I—"

"And we could go camping," Andi continued. "You, me and dad. We could take you to Badger's Crossing and you could see the place for yourself and—"

"I don't think you're going to be up for camping anytime soon," Will said, squeezing Andi's hand gently. "And—" as much as he hated to acknowledge it "—Taylor probably has plans to travel to another location. She wasn't exactly on vacation during our trip—she was working."

The excitement shining in Andi's eyes dimmed and she nodded reluctantly. "I know. It'd just be nice to do something together again—without the drama," she added on a small laugh. She looked at Taylor again and issued a sad smile. "I understand if you can't stay. For a second, I just thought maybe—"

"You have any good fishing holes around here?" Taylor asked, leaning forward and propping her elbows on her knees.

"Yeah," Andi said. "At least a dozen."

"Any waterfalls near these fishing holes?"

"Tons." Andi perked up, planted her hands on the mattress and shimmied upright a couple of inches. "And there are really great views of rapids from the banks of the river near our house. I could show you all of the best places. You'd have enough great shots to sell to at least ten magazines."

Taylor pondered this, tapping her chin with her fingertip. "What about hotels? You know of any good places to stay that'll have a reasonable rent for a couple weeks? I have to be careful. Can't afford a suite with a Jacuzzi on the pay from my photo gigs."

"A Jacuzzi?" Will tilted his head and grinned.

"I'll tell you later." She smiled, the excited gleam in her eye coaxing a surge of affection within him. "Would you mind if I stayed a little while longer? Hung around you two for an extended work-vacation?"

"No," Will said softly, his voice catching with happiness. "I wouldn't mind at all." He held her gaze for a moment longer. Then, catching Andi's eyes on them, he cleared his throat. "Guess I'll go check on those cheeseburgers."

"Would you bring us back some more cherry sodas?" Andi asked, her smile wide.

He motioned toward the can in Taylor's hand. "You haven't finished the one Taylor brought you yet."

"But I will." When he raised his eyebrow, she shrugged. "Dad, we've all been deprived. You eat three cheeseburgers and I'll drink two cherry sodas."

"Guess you got a point." Smiling, he opened the door, but he stopped abruptly, inches from the nurse who was entering the room.

The nurse glanced at Taylor, then frowned at Will. "Visiting hours are over. Only family members are allowed."

Will moved to speak, but Andi beat him to it.

"Taylor is family," she said, grabbing Taylor's hand as she made to rise from her chair.

Will met Taylor's eyes and the same surge of affection sweeping through him was reflected in her eyes. "Yeah," he affirmed. "Taylor's family."

Epilogue

Taylor lifted her camera, zoomed in at just the right angle and said, "Smile as though you spent several days stranded in mountain backcountry and just spotted a rescue helicopter in the distance."

Andi, standing on a popular overlook in the Great Smoky Mountains National Park, propped her hands on her hips and laughed. Will slung his arm around Andi's shoulders and grinned, his handsome features proud as he looked at his daughter.

"Or," Taylor added, snapping another photo of father and daughter beneath the bright summer sun, "smile as though you just graduated from high school."

Andi threw her arms out wide and tossed back her head, her long brown hair rippling in the breeze.

Hours earlier, she and Will, dressed in their Sunday best, had sat in the bleachers of Stone Creek High School's football stadium on a Saturday morning and cheered Andi on as she'd walked across the stage and received her diploma. Taylor had run out of tissues to mop up her tears of joy, and even though he'd tried to hide it, Will's eyes had glistened in the early-morning sunlight as he'd watched his daughter, elegantly dressed in her cap and gown and heels, stride confidently off the stage and back to her seat, waving at him in the stands along the way.

It had been slow going one year ago as Will and Andi had rebuilt the trust between them. After leaving the hospital, Andi had been eager to go home—something that had surprised, and pleased, Will more than he'd been comfortable admitting to Andi. But he'd shared his joy with Taylor, and she'd delighted in watching Will and Andi's bond renew over the three weeks she'd spent renting a motel room in Stone Creek and touring the local fishing holes with them both.

Taylor smiled as she moved a few steps to the left for a different angle and snapped several more pictures of Will and Andi. She'd loved every minute of the three weeks she'd spent with Will and Andi a year ago…and she'd fallen more in love with Will every day that had followed.

She'd exchanged the motel room for an apartment and relocated to Stone Creek, spending her free time with Will and Andi and taking Andi along with her on photography gigs whenever possible. Andi was a quick learner and had a natural talent with the camera. Over the ensuing months, she and Will had grown closer, taking Andi on rafting and camping trips, cooking evening meals together at his house and sitting outside under the moonlight, admiring the stars and recalling moments from the trip down Bear's Tooth

River that had changed the course of their lives in the best ways possible.

"Now, you two," Andi said, jogging across the grassy overlook and reaching for the camera. "Let me take a few of you."

Taylor hesitated as she handed Andi the camera. "But it's your day, Andi. The purpose of this camping trip is to celebrate your achievements. I'm putting together a portfolio for you, and I want a lot of pictures of you and your dad to—"

"And I want a lot of pictures of the two of you," she stated firmly, giving Taylor a gentle nudge. "Now, get over there and practice your smile."

Taylor laughed as she joined Will. "Would you look at that? She graduates high school and thinks she's the boss now."

"I am the boss," Andi teased, grinning. "At least for the weekend. Then my celebration is over and it's back to normal." She snapped a picture, then paused. "Or a new normal, rather, seeing as how I've decided to attend Tennessee State in the fall."

"Oh, that's wonderful," Taylor said, smiling up at Will. "Why didn't you tell me? You knew I was anxious about that." She glanced at Andi. "I was hoping you'd decide to stay in state so you could visit more often."

Andi grinned, a suspicious light sparkling in her eyes. "Oh, I plan on sticking close to home this summer."

"Then we can take that rafting trip we've been planning." Taylor began an itinerary in her mind, listing all the locations she'd planned to photograph along the trip. "I really want to get some shots of the falls near—"

"I hope we'll be too busy for a rafting trip," Will said, wrapping his arms around Taylor's waist and drawing her close.

Andi continued snapping pictures, the soft clicks of the camera repeating rapidly in the background.

Taylor frowned up at Will. "What do you mean?"

"I mean that I'm hoping that we'll be too busy planning our wedding to take a rafting trip," Will said softly.

Taylor stilled, her breath catching as she searched his eyes.

He smiled down at her, his expression softening as he opened his palm. A diamond ring glittered in the sunlight and tears of happiness flooded her eyes.

"I love you, Taylor," he whispered. "And I can't imagine my future without you in it."

The soft snick of the camera continued, and Taylor, tears of joy streaming down her face, glanced at Andi. "You knew about this, didn't you?"

Andi smiled, her own eyes glistening. "Yes. And I fully expect to be your maid of honor."

Taylor laughed. "I wouldn't have it any other way."

"Does this mean you're saying yes?" Will asked, cradling her face in his hands and wiping away her tears.

"Yes," she whispered. "I love you, Will."

He kissed her softly, right there on the overlook beneath the wide sky, amid the impressive mountain range. Moments later, Andi propped the camera on a large boulder, set the timer and joined them on the overlook, wrapping an arm around each of their waists and smiling into the camera as it clicked, snapping a picture—the first of many for a new family full of faith and love.

* * * * *

Get 4 FREE REWARDS!
We'll send you 2 FREE Books
plus 2 FREE Mystery Gifts.
LOVE INSPIRED SUSPENSE
INSPIRATIONAL ROMANCE
Evidence of Innocence
SHIRLEE McCOY
LARGER PRINT
LOVE INSPIRED SUSPENSE
INSPIRATIONAL ROMANCE
Alaskan Rescue
TERRI REED
ALASKA K-9 UNIT
LARGER PRINT
Love Inspired Suspense books showcase how courage and optimism unite in stories of faith and love in the face of danger.
FREE Value Over $20
YES! Please send me 2 FREE Love Inspired Suspense novels and my 2 FREE mystery gifts (gifts are worth about $10 retail). After receiving them, if I don't wish to receive any more books, I can return the shipping statement marked "cancel." If I don't cancel, I will receive 6 brand-new novels every month and be billed just $5.24 each for the regular-print edition or $5.99 each for the larger-print edition in the U.S., or $5.74 each for the regular-print edition or $6.24 each for the larger-print edition in Canada. That's a savings of at least 13% off the cover price. It's quite a bargain! Shipping and handling is just 50¢ per book in the U.S. and $1.25 per book in Canada.* I understand that accepting the 2 free books and gifts places me under no obligation to buy anything. I can always return a shipment and cancel at any time. The free books and gifts are mine to keep no matter what I decide.
Choose one: ☐ Love Inspired Suspense Regular-Print (153/353 IDN GNWN) ☐ Love Inspired Suspense Larger-Print (107/307 IDN GNWN)
Name (please print)
Address
Apt. #
City
State/Province
Zip/Postal Code
Email: Please check this box ☐ if you would like to receive newsletters and promotional emails from Harlequin Enterprises ULC and its affiliates. You can unsubscribe anytime.
Mail to the Harlequin Reader Service:
IN U.S.A.: P.O. Box 1341, Buffalo, NY 14240-8531
IN CANADA: P.O. Box 603, Fort Erie, Ontario L2A 5X3
Want to try 2 free books from another series? Call 1-800-873-8635 or visit www.ReaderService.com.
*Terms and prices subject to change without notice. Prices do not include sales taxes, which will be charged (if applicable) based on your state or country of residence. Canadian residents will be charged applicable taxes. Offer not valid in Quebec. This offer is limited to one order per household. Books received may not be as shown. Not valid for current subscribers to Love Inspired Suspense books. All orders subject to approval. Credit or debit balances in a customer's account(s) may be offset by any other outstanding balance owed by or to the customer. Please allow 4 to 6 weeks for delivery. Offer available while quantities last.
Your Privacy—Your information is being collected by Harlequin Enterprises ULC, operating as Harlequin Reader Service. For a complete summary of the information we collect, how we use this information and to whom it is disclosed, please visit our privacy notice located at corporate.harlequin.com/privacy-notice. From time to time we may also exchange your personal information with reputable third parties. If you wish to opt out of this sharing of your personal information, please visit readerservice.com/consumerschoice or call 1-800-873-8635. Notice to California Residents—Under California law, you have specific rights to control and access your data. For more information on these rights and how to exercise them, visit corporate.harlequin.com/california-privacy.
LIS21R2

Out horseback riding, Dr. Katherine Gilroy accidentally stumbles into a deadly shoot-out and comes to US marshal Dominic O'Ryan's aid. Now with Dominic injured and under her care, she's determined to help him find the fugitive who killed his partner...before they both end up dead.

Read on for a sneak preview of Mountain Fugitive *by Lynette Eason, available October 2021 from Love Inspired Suspense.*

Katherine placed a hand on his shoulder. "Don't move," she said.

He blinked and she caught a glimpse of sapphire-blue eyes. He let out another groan.

"Just stay still and let me look at your head."

"I'm fine." He rolled to his side and he squinted up at her. "Who're you?"

"I'm Dr. Katherine Gilroy, so I think I'm the better judge of whether or not you're fine. You have a head wound, which means possible concussion." She reached for him. "What's your name?"

He pushed her hand away. "Dominic O'Ryan. A branch caught me. Knocked me loopy for a few seconds, but not out. We were running from the shooter." His eyes sharpened. "He's still out there." His hand went to his right hip, gripping the empty holster next to the badge on his belt. A star within a circle. “Where’s my gun? Where’s Carl? My partner, Carl Manning. We need to get out of here.”

“I’m sorry,” Katherine said, her voice soft. “He didn’t make it.”

He froze. Then horror sent his eyes wide—and searching. They found the man behind her and Dominic shuddered.

After a few seconds, he let out a low cry, then sucked in another deep breath and composed his features. The intense moment lasted only a few seconds, but Katherine knew he was compartmentalizing, stuffing his emotions into a place he could hold them and deal with them later.

She knew because she’d often done the same thing. Still did on occasion.

In spite of that, his grief was palpable, and Katherine’s heart thudded with sympathy for him. She moved back to give him some privacy, her eyes sweeping the hills around them once more. Again, she saw nothing, but the hairs on the back of her neck were standing straight up. “I think we need to find some better cover.”

As if to prove her point, another crack sounded. Katherine grabbed the first-aid kit with one hand and pulled Dominic to his feet with the other. “Run!”

LISEXP0921